LIFE AFTER

LIFE AFTER

SARAH ANNE CARTER

www.blkdogpublishing.com

CHAPTER ONE

Amber liked to remember.

She remembered the taste of chocolate chip cookie dough ice cream.

She remembered the warmth of a hot shower after soccer practice.

She remembered laughing at her favorite shows on television after school.

She remembered spending hours shopping at the mall for clothes she could alter to fit her own style.

In the beginning, everyone liked to listen to her stories. She would describe every detail from her memories and when she was done, most people had their eyes closed and were lost in their own memories. She was always willing to stop what she was doing and share her memories with anyone who wanted to listen.

But very quickly, as this new life became more desperate, fewer and fewer people asked her to share her stories. They didn't want to remember how wonderful and easy life used to be for them.

Even her parents snapped at her one night during that first winter when they were all huddled together under eight blankets in one bed, hungry and worried that the storm howling outside would knock the neighbor's tree down on their roof. She was talking about coming inside after playing out in the snow to a warm house, eating cookies fresh out of the oven and drinking hot chocolate with marshmallows. She was describing the smell of the cookies when Mom spoke up on the other side of the bed.

"Amber, stop talking! We can't live in the past. And we all need to sleep."

Amber made eye contact with her brother, Christopher, who gave her a half-hearted smile as he shivered. Maybe he would still want to hear her stories when their parents weren't around. She rolled over to face the wall and stopped talking. She suddenly felt cold all over and a tear slipped down her cheek.

There would be no hot chocolate this winter. No cookies. No warm house.

There was no power – and there hadn't been for months.

CHAPTER TWO

The car hit a pothole and Amber almost dropped the sketches she had made during church. She had drawn them in the margins of the bulletin they had picked up on their way into church, but Amber had forgotten to pace herself and had used every blank space before the sermon even started. She had some really good ideas for how to transform the dress she was wearing into something she would actually enjoy wearing.

Amber was wearing a lilac dress with deep purple flowers all over it and a deep purple trim at the bottom. It had short sleeves and an A-line skirt. She would need to buy some more fabric paint and purple camouflage fabric this week before she started altering the dress. She wished she had thought to bring her sketchbook for the car ride but she wasn't used to going to church. Their family usually only went twice a year and one time was Easter. As her mother told a friend when she picked up Amber from art club on Friday, they weren't "particularly religious, but it didn't feel right not to go to church on Easter and Christmas." She needed to sketch out the dress in a few different lengths before she decided what looked best. Or maybe she could make some leggings to go with it, she thought.

Amber was the only one in her family who got excited about going to church on Easter and Christmas. It was only because it meant she could get a new dress to alter. She had gone shopping with her mother two weeks ago and they had visited four stores before she had found a dress that both her mother liked and Amber would wear in public. She was one store away from not getting a new dress at all by that point, her mother had threatened. Amber always had to promise she wouldn't alter the dress until after she had worn it to church. Hardly any item of clothing in her room was in its original condition. She had been adding her own flair to her wardrobe since learning how to use a sewing machine three years ago. Her grandmother had given it to her on her twelfth birthday, along with lessons at a local store as an early Christmas present. Grandma Birch was the only grandparent Amber had gotten to know well since the other three had passed away when she was young. Grandma Birch had lived in a townhouse in a community for "golden people," as she called it, about an hour away and they had seen her often.

"I want you to make me something colorful and bright to add to my wardrobe," Grandma Birch had asked after Amber gave her a thank you hug. "The clothes they make for folks my age tend to be so boring compared to what you young ones wear. You know I love colors!" Grandma Birch wore colorful clothing as much as she could and, even though her hair was white, she kept it long when most women her age had short hair, which made her seem younger than she was to Amber.

The day after her birthday that year, Amber begged Mom to take her to the craft store. She didn't have much time, but wanted to make a scarf and reversible bag for Grandma for Christmas. Amber chose purple and yellow fabrics for the bag and found a fun polka-dot fabric for the scarf.

Grandma Birch passed away from a stroke just a week after Amber gave her the gifts for Christmas. She had been buried in a plain navy blue suit, but Amber had snuck the scarf she had made around her neck when it was her turn to pay her respects. Her mother had seen and had smiled at her and nodded. She was sure Grandma had smiled at that, too.

"Amber, remember this year you need to help hide the eggs," her mom said as they pulled into their driveway, pulling Amber back to reality. "You're too old to be finding them – even if there are passes to the movies."

"Are you sure, Mom? That new *Prince Valiant* movie is coming out next month," she said as she got out. Her mom laughed at her as she slammed the door and ran through the garage and into house. She needed to get out of the dress and into her own clothes. The dress would be so much more comfortable to wear after she fixed it up. She picked out khaki capris that now had hot pink pockets and trim at the bottom of the legs and a purple shirt that been tie-dyed with bleach. She pulled her wavy brown hair up into a ponytail since her mother had forced her to wear it down for church. Within five minutes she was back out the front door to go look for her friend and neighbor, Alex, so they could hide the eggs for the annual neighborhood Easter Egg Hunt.

Last year, Amber and Alex had been outside kicking a soccer ball around when Mrs. Allen, the neighborhood Homeowners' Association President, had started hiding eggs for her children and their friends, still in her church clothes and high heels, although her blond hair was up in a ponytail. They had offered to help her after seeing her high heels get stuck in the grass a few times. Then they had to help the children find the ones that were hidden really well. Mrs. Allen had let them keep a few eggs for themselves.

"Amber! Alex!" she called as they were waiting for the school bus in the morning two weeks ago. "I have a question for you."

"Everything okay, Mrs. Allen?" Amber asked.

"Oh, yes," she said. "I was just wondering if you two could organize the Easter Egg Hunt for the neighborhood this year. I already have all the eggs, candy and prizes. You guys did such a good job last year and I'll be busy that day getting a big meal ready. It's our turn to host for our family."

"That sounds like fun," Amber said.

"The kids loved it last year," Alex said.

"It'll be a new Trebein Trails tradition," Mrs. Allen said. "Thank you. I'll bring the stuff over next week."

Their neighborhood, located on Treibein Trails Drive, was only three years old. Tucked away near Asheville, North Carolina, it was a "No Outlet" neighborhood built around a small playground and grassy area with a gazebo, making a rectangle shape. It was supposed to be a small part of a large, new suburban housing subdivision, Adelaide Acres, but after the houses on Treibein Trails were built, the building company went bankrupt, along with many others that year, and there were only a few paved lots up the street that would suggest more houses were supposed to be built. Otherwise, it was just a neighborhood tucked away among some farm fields. Amber had heard her parents talking about how the owners of the few surrounding farms had tried to bring a lawsuit against the building company since the farmers had been promised by the company to be bought out, but nothing ever came from it, except that those farmers now regarded the neighborhood as an eyesore. School was only a ten-minute drive away and there were a few houses on land scattered along that drive. The grocery store was a twenty-minute drive, but it was located next to a few strip malls with enough stores and restaurants to keep the teenagers happy. It was a forty-five-minute drive to Asheville where there was a mall and movie theater. Amber was looking forward to getting her driving permit in a few months. She had plans to go to the mall a lot once a driver's license was in her wallet. There were three fabric and craft stores down by the mall. There was only a small craft store in the nearby strip mall and Amber usually spent most of her allowance there. The owner, Trina, knew her by name and Amber was planning to ask her for a job there this summer. It was the same store where she took the sewing lessons Grandma bought her to go along with the sewing machine. Trina often held crafting classes in the evenings at the store.

As Amber opened her door to head outside, she saw Alex was already at the playground. He was wearing his typical outfit of running shorts and a Tennessee Titans T-shirt. Alex's and her houses both faced the playground and neighborhood entrance. They were in the same grade in school and had been friends before their families moved into the new neighborhood, although they had only seen each other at school back then since they lived on different sides of town. Alex was a mere two months older than Amber. They had known each other as classmates, but finally talked during a fifth grade gym class where they were both sitting on the sidelines during a soccer game. Alex had broken his arm from falling off his bicycle and she had twisted her ankle tripping over her brother's toy trucks in the living room. Alex started calling plays like a sports announcer and Amber joined in. They ended up in the same class in sixth grade and made sure to sign up for the same gym classes in middle school.

"You're late again. I already got the eggs from my basement," Alex shouted at her.

"I wouldn't be late if we didn't have to go to church like you," she retorted as soon as she got close enough so she wouldn't have to yell.

"You know you still would," he said, laughing. He handed her a bag and they started hiding the eggs. The neighborhood children started lining up on the sidewalk. The children started asking Amber and Alex questions.

"Are you done yet?" "Can we go?" "Is there chocolate?" "What's in the sparkly egg?" "That one is mine!" They both started walking slower with each question. When they were done hiding the eggs, Alex came to where Amber was standing and started whispering to her.

"Should we make them wait longer?"

"I don't know. Maybe it's been long enough."

"Oh, I have an idea," Alex whispered and started walking toward the children.

"Before we start the annual Trebein Trails Egg Hunt, I'd like to talk to you about safety," Alex said to the kids. There were a few groans.

"Rule one is to run. Don't walk, run. Rule two is to look out for yourself and get as many eggs as you can." The kids started laughing. "Rule three is to ... Go!"

The children started scrambling for the eggs. Amber smiled. Alex would be a good teacher if he wanted to be one like her, but he wanted to be an auto mechanic. His dad had bought him a broken-down motorcycle for his birthday in January, promising him that he could drive it if he could get it to work. Alex spent at least an hour after school each day working on it. He said his mom threatened to put it in storage if he got any grease on her new couch.

Amber took a minute to just watch the children and enjoy the sunshine. The egg hunt was finished in less than five minutes. There was a light breeze, but it was warm for that time of year. Despite the heat, most of the adults gathered near the children at the playground who were swapping candy and setting up another egg hunt with the goodies from the first egg hunt. The past week had been pretty cloudy and rainy, so they were enjoying being able to be outside.

Alex and Amber kicked a soccer ball around for a while and then Alex left to go check the score of the baseball game. Amber stayed out with the children helping them set up egg hunt after egg hunt. When she looked around after taking a break, she saw Alex standing by a group of adults at the far end of the playground. She knew her mom had been planning to spend the afternoon making pies and cooking a ham dinner, but both her parents were in the group. She walked over to see what was going on.

"Why won't my phone work?" she heard Shelley ask her mom, Mrs. Jensen. Shelley was a year ahead of her in school.

"I don't know. Mine won't either," Mrs. Jensen replied.

"It's just not a normal power outage," Amber heard her dad say.

"Tell me about it," Mr. Reed said. "Neither one of my cars will start."

"My generator hasn't kicked on either and it hasn't failed us before," Mrs. Allen said. "I was hoping it would start up so my cake could finish baking."

"I bet a car hit one of the poles nearby," Amber's mom said. "That's usually why the power goes out. I bet it'll be back on in just an hour or two."

"But why can't I even call the power company to see?" Alex's mom, Mrs. McCarthy, asked. "The landline doesn't work and no one's cell phone works either."

"Maybe power was cut to the cell tower?" Mr. Jensen guessed.

"The phone would still be on if that were true," Mr. McCarthy said.

"It's all very strange," Amber's mom said, almost in a whisper.

Alex came and stood by her.

"This stinks," he said. "I really wanted to watch the Pirates game this afternoon."

"I was hoping to do some sewing," she replied. "Guess I'll just do some sketches or read instead."

"Wait, want to see if Shelley and Susanna want to play UNO? We could set it up on my back porch in the shade."

"That would be fun. I'll go ask them if you get it set up."

They played until dinnertime when their parents came to get them. The power was still out.

CHAPTER THREE

"Well, we're not having ham for Easter dinner this year," Mom told Amber said as she returned home. There was a collection of candles on the kitchen counter. Her mother must have gathered them from all around the house.

"Does that mean I can't have apple pie?" Christopher asked, sighing.

"Well, no pie, but you can have ice cream," she replied.

"Wait, Christopher, don't open the freezer yet," their dad said as Christopher headed toward the refrigerator. "We're only going to open those doors each once tonight. I'm going to grill burgers so we need to get those out when we get the ice cream."

"Well, I want to put the cheese and milk in the freezer to keep those cold, so let's open the fridge first," their mom said.

Her parents moved the food items and took out what they needed for dinner. They handed Amber and Christopher the burger patties, ice cream, corn on the cob and butter to put on the kitchen counter. As soon as they closed the door, Amber realized they had forgotten to take out the ketchup, mustard and pickles. As much as she and Christopher begged, their dad wouldn't relent and told them they would have to have burgers without the condiments.

"I know a burger's not the same without ketchup, but as a consolation, that ice cream is not going back in the freezer so if you want to start eating it as your appetizer, go right ahead," he said.

Amber and Christopher started scooping the ice cream into bowls right away and ate them at the kitchen counter while their parents took the burgers out on the deck to grill them.

When her dad came back in to wash his hands after putting the burgers on the grill, the faucet sputtered to a stop right after he put the soap on his hands.

"Dang it! I always forget about that," he said. Every house in the neighborhood got water from a well, which ran on an electric well pump – no power meant there was no running water. Last year, Amber was running a bath to soak her legs after a grueling soccer practice and the power went out when the bath was only half full. She waited two hours and just as she finally got into bed for the night, the power came back on. Most homes had whole-house generators put in just for that one reason. However, they didn't have one and from what their neighbors had said, no one's generator was working right now anyway.

"Amber, get a case of water from the basement and help me rinse the soap off my hands," he said. His voice was low, which was always a sign of him feeling stressed. They usually stayed out of their dad's way when his voice got like that. Amber quickly put her ice cream bowl down on the counter and went downstairs to get the case of water. Their cat, Miss Gray, ran down the stairs as soon as Amber opened the door. Instinctively, she reached up for the pull-string to turn on the light, but, of course, nothing happened. She found the storage room door with the faint light from the top of the stairs, opened it and felt for the cases of water on the floor. Her family kept bulk food and household purchases in the basement. Her mom liked a good bargain, so if buying a year's worth of toilet paper meant that it was cheaper in the long run, she couldn't pass it up. She had once started a blog called Saving Sherrie, but never found the time to keep it going consistently. She told her friends more than once that she had lost her opportunity since money-saving blogs were really popular now. Amber left the storage door open since she didn't know where Miss Gray was and hurried to take the case upstairs.

She put the case on the kitchen table and got a bottle to pour water over dad's hands.

"Just use a little bit," he said, his voice still low. "We'll need to conserve water until we know what exactly is going on."

"It's just a power outage, right?" she asked. Her mom was sitting at the table near the kitchen staring at a small bowl of ice cream.

"If it's normal, then why can't I play on my tablet? It was on the charger all morning," Christopher said.

"Umm … I'm not sure. I need to check on the burgers. Sherrie, can you come help me?" Amber's parents shut the glass door to the deck behind them as they left the house.

"Don't you realize you'll hear more if you stay quiet when adults talk than if you ask questions?" Amber asked her brother. He was only nine and stuck his tongue out at her before he took his ice cream bowl from the kitchen to the living room. She turned back to finish her ice cream and saw that he had eaten hers while she had been in the basement.

"Brothers," she muttered under her breath. She wondered why her dad was so stressed about this power outage. Did he think something else was going on?

Her parents didn't talk much during the late dinner, so Amber and Christopher kept pretty quiet, too. They ate the plain burgers out on the back deck, like most of the neighborhood. The sun was starting to get low and candles and flashlights were lighting up the backyards. Normally, voices would echo across the lawns, but tonight the wind just brought whispers. It had been about six hours with no power and Amber was starting to worry, especially since there didn't seem to be a cause like a thunderstorm or high winds. It was more like an outage than just a power outage – no power, no cell phones, no Internet, no cars, no phone landlines.

"Let's go inside and talk," her dad said. They gathered their paper plates and plastic utensils and took them inside. Her mom lit one candle and put it on the table.

"Don't throw your trash away, kids," he said. "Put it on the counter for now. We want to talk to you guys."

He motioned for them to sit down at the table. Amber

sat down next to her mom and Christopher sat at her other side. Dad stood up. He liked to be on his feet when he was talking.

"So, your mom and I think this situation feels a little strange. We really don't know why cars and phones aren't working along with having no power," he said.

"I've rarely heard of any power outage lasting more than a few days, so I think we should plan for that," Mom said. "However, with big disasters, there have been outages up to a month."

"Big disasters?" Amber asked.

"Like wildfires, earthquakes and floods," she replied.

"But we didn't …" her brother interrupted.

"We didn't here," Dad said, "but there may have been something a few counties over or in a nearby state. There once was an earthquake in Missouri big enough to make the Mississippi flow backwards. I'm guessing it must have been something big to take out the Internet and landlines, too.

"The longest outage I've ever seen was two days due to a blizzard when I was in college. That was actually kind of fun. Everyone in the dorm brought their food down to the common room and we shared."

"I've never seen it out for more than a few hours," Mom added. "It'll probably be back on when we wake up in the morning. It really can't go on for very long. You guys shouldn't worry, though. We will take care of you and we'll figure all this out. It will be like a family adventure."

"If this is anything like our last camping adventure, you mean this will be a lot of work," Amber said and crossed her arms.

"Amber Carrisa Birch!" her mom scolded.

"It's okay, Sherrie," he said, putting his hand on her arm. "You're right, Amber, it may be a lot of work, but if this does turn out to be an adventure, guess where you won't be going on Monday – school."

Amber uncrossed her arms and smiled. She thought about having no school, no tests, no studying.

"Really? No school?" Amber asked.

"If the cars don't work, the school buses won't work either. I don't even know what time it is for you to go out and wait for the bus. We'll know for sure in the morning, though – with how quiet it is, we'll definitely hear if the school bus comes by."

"I want to go to school!" Christopher said. He looked down at his wrist. "I know the time. My watch says it's 8:28."

"It's okay, Christopher, we can do school stuff at home," Mom said.

"But I'll miss Timmy and Blake … and Mr. Stuffy. It's finally my turn to feed Mr. Stuffy this week. Remember I had to switch my week, I was supposed to have him last week, but Suzy was going to Florida this week and Ms. Martin made me switch with her," Christopher said as he started sniffling. Mr. Stuffy was the class hamster and Christopher had been look-ing forward to his turn for months. Amber called him a crybaby in her head, but knew better than to say it out loud.

"Christopher, come with me and we'll start to get ready for bed. Amber, help your father clean up," Mom said as she guided Christopher toward the stairs.

Amber's dad sent her out with a flashlight to make sure the propane was turned off on the grill and everything was cleaned up outside. She came in to find him muttering to himself while staring at the plates.

"If I only knew how long …"

"How long what?" she asked him.

He looked up at her and she could tell he was forcing himself to smile.

"Oh, I'm just talking to myself. I knew we should have started the compost last year," he opened the door to their trash and recycle can and sighed. "I guess I'll just put it all in the trash for now."

Amber helped her dad with the trash and then asked to get ready for bed. Dad gave her one bottle of water to brush her teeth – "just use a little" – and reminded her to take the flashlight with her.

"Oh, I forgot about Miss Gray!" She took the flashlight off the kitchen counter and ran all the way down to the basement. She could hear the faint meowing from the storage room. She snatched up Miss Gray and nuzzled her. The cat usually slept in Amber's bed at night.

After giving the cat a treat and taking the bottle of water from the kitchen counter, she walked up the stairs and went up to her bedroom. Her mom met her at the top of the stairs.

"Bed already?"

"Well, there's no TV to watch tonight. I guess I'll write in my journal then read."

"Okay – goodnight."

"Goodnight, Mom."

Amber went to her room and shut the door. She pulled her journal out from under her mattress. She started writing down the day's events and fell asleep before she finished. She'd regret it in the morning when she realized her flashlight batteries were dead from being on all night and the power was still out.

CHAPTER FOUR

The weather was nice the next two days and Amber spent most of the day outside with Alex. Their parents were spending a lot of time together, but always stopped talking when she walked anywhere near them. Amber knew they were talking about the power outage and she knew something strange had to be going on for them to not want her to hear.

"I bet they're talking about food," Alex said when he caught her staring at their parents on her front porch on Tuesday.

"I bet you're right. Have you heard your parents say anything? Mine won't even whisper if Christopher or I am around them," she asked him.

"I overheard them say Mr. Jackson had someone knock at his door yesterday asking for some water. They had been up at the Savers Mart getting some groceries when the power went out. His car wouldn't work but he waited there for a while hoping it would come back on. He started walking home Sunday night, but didn't want to keep going in the dark so he turned back and waited until Monday morning. He was headed to the neighborhood by the school, so our neighborhood was about halfway for him. My mom said something about a 20-minute driving taking almost five hours to walk."

"I wonder if we'll see any more people walking home," Amber said.

"Probably. Can you imagine walking to the mall?" he

said as he shook his head. "The power has to come back on tomorrow, don't you think?"

"I hope so," Amber said.

Amber's mom would let them get a little bit of milk for their cereal at breakfast and then she would hurriedly take out whatever she thought they might need for the day from the refrigerator and freezer. If the doors stayed shut, the items would stay cold, even frozen, for a few days. The first day was hot dogs with no buns for lunch and grilled chicken breasts for dinner. The second day they had taco meat salads for lunch and pork chops for dinner.

On the morning of the third day, her mom put everything from the refrigerator in the freezer that needed to stay cold and took out another pack of hot dogs and chicken breasts.

"I don't have that much meat left," Amber heard her mom say under her breath. If they power didn't come back on, Amber realized there wouldn't be any place to get fresh food. Maybe they could get some canned goods from the Savers Mart, but otherwise, they only had the food that was left in their house – unless their neighbor's shared.

It was rainy on the third full day with no power. Amber's family was playing their second round of Monopoly for the day to pass the time when there was a knock at the door. Amber got up to see who it was, hoping it was Alex about some plans for an afternoon session of board games with Susanna and Shelley.

"Oh, hello, Mrs. Allen."

"Is your father home, Amber?" Amber could only guess Mrs. Allen was on Homeowner's Association business. Her dad was the vice president.

"Come on in, Cathy," Dad called from the living room. They usually played board games in their formal dining room, but there was only a small window in that room and since it was cloudy that day, they needed to be in a room with windows to play to have more light. They had set up the game on the coffee table and put stacks of pillows around to sit on.

Amber closed the door and followed Mrs. Allen into the

living room. She was holding a notebook with a pen clipped on it.

"I thought it might be good to go to each house and see how everyone is doing. It's so strange to me that we're on day three of no power and no way to know why. I was wondering if you'd want to split them up between us and then meet back up and discuss any problems."

"That's sounds like a really good idea," he said.

"I could go, too, to make it quicker," her mom offered.

"That would be wonderful," Mrs. Allen said. "I'll do my street if you do yours and the two side streets. My husband is home watching the kids. I know the Alexanders went out of town this weekend, but I don't know if they asked someone to watch their dog or if they put it in a kennel. I haven't seen Copper roaming around like he normally does. I may have to break a lock or window to find out."

"You should take Alex with you," Amber spoke up. "He's been fixing his motorcycle and might have some tools that could help with a lock."

"That's a great idea," Mrs. Allen said. "I'll stop by his house before I head to the Alexanders' house."

"Why don't we meet back here around dinnertime and you bring your family? We have some chicken that is still good that I can put on the grill."

When Mrs. Allen left, Amber and Christopher asked if they could come along. Her parents told them no and asked them to stay inside until they got back. Her mom found some notebooks and pens at the office nook by the kitchen and then they headed out.

"Want to play Trouble?" Christopher asked her.

"No, I'm going to read," Amber said. She couldn't read as much at night anymore after she burned through her flashlight batteries on the first night. Her parents limited her time with the flashlight at night and that included getting ready for bed. Her parents would check on her before they went to bed to make sure she had turned the flashlight off.

"Do you think everyone in the neighborhood is okay?" he asked before she headed to her bedroom.

"If we stay quiet tonight, we'll probably find out. We're

lucky they didn't send us outside while they talked to Mrs. Allen."

Amber and Christopher were put on babysitting duty watching the Allen kids outside while the parents talked after dinner that night. Christopher was only a year older than Austin, so they played catch while Amber played make-believe princess with six-year-old Ella. When Ella started whining that she couldn't see her unicorn stuffed animals anymore, even though it was a bit on the dramatic side, Amber decided it was dark enough that they should probably head inside. She really wanted to hear what they were saying. They could see the adults had lit some candles already and had the notebooks open on the table where the Monopoly game had been.

Well, at least I was losing that game, Amber thought.

"I think a neighborhood meeting would be a good idea," Amber heard Mrs. Allen say as she opened up the back door. "Let's go back to everyone in the morning and tell them to come to the playground around lunchtime if the power is still off."

"Let's let the Snells and Myers stay home, though," her dad said. "They're elderly and already getting low on their medications and I don't want them getting upset. They were supposed to pick up refills this week."

"That's a good idea. We can tell them about the meeting but then tell them we'll come talk to them afterwards to keep them informed," Mr. Allen said. "We didn't see any signs of the Alexanders' dog. They must have taken Copper with them."

"Mom, my unicorns are tired," Ella declared and climbed into her mother's lap. The boys had gone up to Christopher's room.

"Guess that's enough for one day," Mrs. Allen said. "Thank you both for helping."

"Not a problem," her mom said. "Until the power comes back on, we're all in this together."

The Allens came over shortly after sunrise the next day. Amber and Christopher were asked to watch Austin and Ella again while the adults went around to inform the neighborhood about the meeting. The boys went directly to Christopher's room but Amber got out some construction paper, scissors, glue and crayons and worked with Ella on making a unicorn village. The morning went by quickly and when the adults came home, they worked on an agenda for the meeting in the living room. Amber listened closely to what they said; glad they hadn't sent her away.

"So, maybe we start out by saying we don't know any more than they do, but we want to prepare together in case this goes on for much longer," Mrs. Allen said.

"I think you should try to talk about the safety aspects next," her dad said. "Looks like the Reeds and Polks already had a touch of food poisoning."

"So, there's food safety to discuss, but we also have to talk about sanitation. Without running water, we need to figure out how to get water from the creek in the woods across the street to flush the toilets," her mom said. "A few houses already had a smell to them. They need to add water to them so they'll flush. I guess if it goes on long enough, we'll have to think about outhouses."

"Ugh. It can't go on much longer," Mr. Allen said. "But, if it does, should we discuss pooling food and supplies today or wait?"

"We will have to talk about that soon, but maybe we should just focus on safety items today," her dad said. "I just wish we knew why this was happening."

"We have some bikes in the neighborhood," Mrs. Allen said. "I wouldn't send any of the kids, but maybe one or two of the adults can ride to the closest fire station to see if they can find out any more information."

"That's a good idea," her dad said. "I can go tomorrow. We can ask at the meeting who would like to go with me."

"So, I think it's settled – food safety, sanitation and water," Mrs. Allen said. "Let's get some lunch together for the kids and then head out to the playground."

Amber helped her mom heat up soup that the Allens had brought over in a pot on the grill. They had some crackers to go with it and cut up an apple so everyone could have one slice. Amber thought about where they might put an outhouse. She didn't really want to have to go outside to use the bathroom, but she knew people did that for years and years. There was starting to be an odor in the house from them not flushing the toilet more than once a day since they had to use their water to do it. Her dad tried to have them use the dishwater, but last night, Amber forgot and used bottled water. The look on Dad's face was all she needed to see to make sure she didn't do that again. For dishes, they heated water on the grill, filled the sink with that and soap and then washed. A rag with a tiny bit of water on it was what they used to rinse them off. Every little thing they had to do seemed so much harder to Amber without electricity – and much more time-consuming. She was thinking of starting to hand-stitch together a blanket out of fabric scraps she had left over, just to have something to do. She usually had a few sewing projects going on since it was relaxing for her to sew. With no machine to use, those projects seemed daunting now. Hand stitching would take a long time, but she had to be creative somehow.

Amber's family and the Allens were the first ones at the playground, but then each family slowly started emerging from their houses. Alex's family was next and Alex was kicking his soccer ball on his way to the playground. He nodded toward the grassy area beside the small gazebo and she met them there.

"Do you know that they're going to talk about? Do they know why the power's out?" he asked her as they started kicking the ball back and forth.

"They don't know. It's so strange. They're going to talk about food safety and water and building outhouses …"

"Outhouses? Ugh."

"I know, but it might be better than the smell starting to come from our bathrooms."

"Good point."

They kicked the ball and listened as the families started to gather. The kids were all heading to the playground. There were just a few clouds in the sky. The adults were gathering near the gazebo and they could hear some of what they were saying, but there were several conversations going on at once. Most of them were talking about food and how and what they'd been cooking and eating.

"There was a time before you were born when the power was out for five days! A tornado ripped through the next county and we had trees down all over the place. I'm sure it'll come back on soon," Amber overhead 8-year-old Mike's Grandma Jenny tell him as they walked up to the playground from behind her. Mike's parents had gone on a trip to Colorado for the Easter weekend and his grandmother had come to watch him. She lived just ten minutes away and had brought her cat with her for the weekend.

"I sure hope it's soon, Grandma," Mike said. "I really want to play my new video game that the Easter bunny left me." Then he ran to the slide.

The other teens in the neighborhood came over to where Amber and Alex were standing. Shelley joined them in kicking the soccer ball but Susanna just stood nearby. Susanna was a senior who was in show choir and performed in the school musical and plays. Shelley was a junior and played soccer, basketball and softball. Amber and Alex were "just" freshmen, as Susanna liked to say, but she was always smiling when she said it.

"Can I have your attention?" Mrs. Allen said as she stood on a bench right outside the gazebo. The crowd quieted except for the children playing. "I have no answers for you right now as to why the power hasn't come back on or why our cars and cell phones aren't working. However, it's important that we come together and help each other out in case we're dealing with a long-term situation.

"We need to be careful about how we're preparing food and figure out the best way to keep our lives sanitary. We also need to create a system to get water from the nearby creek and make sure it's safe to use for drinking, bathing and cooking. In a few minutes, Mr. Birch will go over details on those topics.

"We did want to send out two men out on bikes later today to visit the Ridge Road Fire Station to see if they know anything more about this situation. Mr. Birch has agreed to be one of the men. Is there anyone else who would like to volunteer?"

The crowd was quiet for barely a second before almost everyone started talking. Finally, someone whistled and it was so loud, Amber had to cover her ears. She turned and saw it was Alex.

"Thank you, Alex," her dad said and he stood beside Mrs. Allen on the bench. "Let's just have any interested parties come see me after the meeting. Now that I have your attention back, let me go over some more details and then we'll try to answer any questions, but let's do it by raising hands."

Amber only half-listened as her dad talked about food spoilage and how to make an outhouse since she had heard him talk about it at their house. For a moment, she wondered how he knew about such things and then remembered that he had been an avid hiker when he was in college in Colorado. He had taken a lot of safety classes, including one he called "Woofer," which she remembered was Wilderness First Responder. He had actually used his training a few times during hikes for friends who had minor injuries, but there is the big story when he helped a woman who had gone into premature labor on the trail. He delivered the baby just as the helicopter landed in a field 200 yards away. He ran with the baby and the husband ran with his wife to the helicopter. They both survived, although the baby was in the hospital for weeks. The parents had named her Jacqueline after Jack. He brought out the scrapbook that had the newspaper clippings in it about once a year when they had company over who had never heard the story. Her father still tried to meet up with some college friends once a year for a hike, but he had not been able to go this year due to work.

"There's no way we're using an outhouse!" An angry voice caught Amber's attention. "There is absolutely no way in this day and age that the power will stay out for a long time," said Derrick Sanders. He grabbed onto his wife's arm and they started to walk back home.

A few other couples started to walk away, too, but those who stayed started asking question after question. Her dad and Mrs. Allen had both stepped off the benches and were trying to answer each person one by one. Sherrie and Mr. Allen were getting questions, too.

"It sounds like we're going to be doing a lot of work here, soon," Alex said. "Let's move down towards the kids."

Amber followed him and the older girls stayed behind.

"It's starting to feel like the power is never going to come back on," Amber said. Alex just nodded his head.

The trip to the fire station resulted in the neighborhood gaining one first aid kit and no information. Her father told them at dinner that the station was completely locked up with a note on the door saying they had all gone home to take care of their families since the trucks wouldn't start. There was a pile of first aid kits by the door and the sign had asked people to just take one and leave the rest for others.

"I'm glad Mr. Jackson and I only had to take Beechcraft Road into town and go two blocks down Main," her dad said after telling them about the station. "It was so quiet and we didn't see any people."

"No one at all?" her mom asked.

"No, but there were a few dogs near the fire station and we had to steer around a handful of cars left on the road. I'm guessing most people are just staying home waiting this out."

"If there's no firemen at their station, then there's probably no police at theirs either?" Christopher questioned.

"Probably not," Dad said.

"How do you think the hospital is doing?" Amber asked. The pause was much longer than normal before her mother spoke up.

"We can only hope and pray that their generators are working. If not, it wouldn't be good."

They were all silent for the remainder of dinner that night. Then her dad broke the silence by announcing he was going to show them all how to divide up the trash. They would give any meat scraps to the cat and then the rest of the food and paper would be composted or be burned unless it was something that could be washed and be used for something else. When in doubt, he said, they needed to ask before throwing something out.

The power was out for three long weeks before they found out why. Almost everything they ate by that point was from a can or box. The fresh produce was all gone and all the meat had been cooked and eaten before it had gone bad. They only used the grill to heat up soup or boil noodles. The propane was eventually going to run out so her dad was trying to fix up their fire pit so they could cook over it.

Several of the men who owned guns were taking turns on "patrol," as Amber's dad liked to call it. During the day, one would sit across the street to watch if anyone was coming their way on the street. At night, the man on patrol watched from the Alexanders' back porch since they still weren't home. So far, they had only seen a handful of people during the day who were offered water from the creek and no one at night.

Amber's next-door neighbor, Mr. Thompson, found a flyer when he was trying to turn part of his lawn into a garden area. It was hard and slow work doing everything with hand tools. Everyone in the neighborhood had finally come to an agreement a few days after the playground meeting about how to work together. Part of the neighborhood agreement was that everyone would put in a garden plot where they each grew a lot of the same thing and then would share the harvest. Even if the power came back on soon, putting in a garden would give them all an extra source of food in case the supply chain took a while to get back to normal. Ivy Snell and Veronica Myers were master gardeners and had a decent supply of seeds at their house and offered most of them to the neighborhood. Amber's family had gotten carrots and potatoes and they were all spending time in the yard digging out the grass. Several pieces of paper blew into Michael's yard and the eagle seal at the top caught his eye, he liked to tell people. He picked one up and read it.

Everyone quickly gathered in the playground area after

hearing his shouts. "There's news! Government news! Every-one come here! News!"

> *My fellow Americans,*
>
> *Please be assured that the U.S. government is still in place and is working to restore power as quickly as possible.*
>
> *The power outage was caused by a massive solar flare that took out power to most of North America. The solar flare also damaged electronic devices. The pockets of this continent that weren't affected, along with several other countries, are working on a plan to help us make parts to replace damaged ones. Our first priority will be power for light, communication and food supplies. We will start doing airdrops of basic supplies throughout the country very soon. Please maintain law and order and help your neighbors as we restore America. People are working around the clock to solve these problems and we may call on people to volunteer as we come to your town.*
>
> *If you are able to get to a military base or indoor shopping mall, we will set up those locations as primary medical and food distribution centers. There will be limited space for sheltering peo-ple, but we will help those that we can.*
>
> *The reality is that it will take us several years to completely restore power. One by one, we will get there.*
>
> *Henry R. Stegner, President of the United States of America*

Everyone in the neighborhood wanted to see the paper with his or her own eyes.

"Years," was the most whispered word. "It could be years." Amber felt the hope slipping away from her. They were facing this new life for a long time. The looks on the faces around her told her other people were feeling the same way.

"We definitely all have to pull together now," her dad said, standing on the bench outside the gazebo again. The whole neighborhood was there and no one seemed to want to leave. "I'm assuming by now that everyone has seen or heard about the letter from the President. If anyone hasn't, can you let me know?"

No one raised their hand or said a word.

"Okay, we all know what has happened and that we'll

be without power for possibly a long time. It's not going to be easy, but I think we have some great people and resources here. However, each family needs to decide what is best for them. If you want to leave and go to the mall for shelter, we can help you prepare for the trip. It was a forty-five-minute drive so I'm thinking it will take you a few days to walk there. We'll need to ask you what things you're leaving behind that we can use for our survival here. Does anyone know yet if they want to leave?"

No one raised their hand, but several shook their heads like they didn't know, but were considering it.

"Okay. Let's have a meeting tomorrow at the same time for those who want to leave. You can stay for this meeting to see how we're going to try and run things.

"For those who want to stay, we have to think more long-term about food, sanitation, security and medical issues. We'll really need to pool together our resources and skills. We're lucky to have the stream that runs through the woods across the street for a water supply. I think we'll need to reach out to some of the surrounding farmers to offer help for food. I need each family to make an updated list of food, medical and gun and ammo supplies. Work on the lists and tomorrow afternoon I want to meet with one member from each family at my home. We will discuss ideas and each member can go back and talk over those ideas and then we'll start making decisions."

Amber noticed there weren't as many questions this time. People seemed serious and thoughtful. She had a terrible feeling in the pit of her stomach. She was a teenager and these were supposed to be the fun years of her life – driving, hanging out with friends at school, going to football games and school dances. Now, she would have to find a way to live without power. She suddenly felt very tired thinking about all the work that lay ahead of them. She walked over to her mom, who gave her a hug.

Three families ended up leaving the neighborhood to head to the mall. The Sanders, Polks and Jacksons headed out just two days after the note was found. The Polks had a 5-year-old girl, Lily, and the Sanders had 8-year-old Ben. The

Jacksons had no children. The Polks and Jacksons signed a paper giving the neighborhood permission to use any of their property and belongings for survival. The Sanders did not. Derrick Sanders said loudly to anyone who would listen that he mainly wanted to go get more food for his wife and son and that he firmly believed the power would be back in a week or two.

CHAPTER FIVE

The days started running together for Amber. In just three months without power, people had lost track of time. The neighborhood had two self-proclaimed timekeepers – Ivy Snell and Veronica Myers – and they each knew for certain what day it was, but they did not agree on what day that was. They were already known to compete in the county fair's gardening contests, but now they were competing about the date. Ivy had a wind-up watch from her grandfather that she had used to keep time since the power went out. She swore she had never let it stop, but her records were two days behind Veronica's. Veronica had been a librarian for forty years. She was a stickler for records and routine. She told everyone that she had kept a journal since she was 15 and swore she had never missed a day.

"Are you sure you didn't take a nap and consider that another day?" Ivy shot at Veronica at one of the neighborhood meetings that almost always ended before it started with the two arguing over the date.

"Nap? You're the one who falls asleep three times a day. There is no way you can be sure that watch never stopped!" Veronica retorted. "It's Thursday – I am sure of it!"

"It is only Tuesday! One day – you will see – I am right!"

"Let me remind you two that the neighborhood has decided to split the difference. It is officially Wednesday in Treibein Trails," Jack said as they called the meeting to order. The neighborhood had a meeting every Wednesday to review the current state of the community. "Not that it matters much anyway," he muttered to himself.

They really only wanted to figure out what day of the week it was so that they could bring order and routine to their lives. For those who were religious, it helped them, and the whole community, to know what day they would have church services. There were also daily and weekly duties the neighborhood had to come together to complete. Patrols and hunting parties went out daily. Trash burning was on Mondays and voluntary sanitation checks were on Fridays. There was usually a case of food poisoning in the neighborhood once a week. It seemed like every person needed to learn the hard way that it was better to be hungry than eat questionable food. Sanitation checks were just a quick peak into each house to make sure food was being contained correctly, check soap levels, see how clean the items were that were used to cook food and make sure the house didn't smell of human waste. Only a few families agreed to let Mrs. Allen and Jack do these, though, and those families didn't really need the inspections. Amber had heard her father tell her mother he was going to bring up dropping them at this meeting.

Amber always hung around when the neighborhood board met, and she usually shared the information she learned with the other teenagers in the neighborhood. She considered herself an ambassador, not a snoop, which her brother liked to call her. Every decision made affected all of them and, in essence, the teens now had very adult-like duties and needed to be informed as to what was going on. Alex did patrol duty every other day. Shelley was on the hunting/scavenging team. Susanna often helped Mrs. Allen with laundry and Amber helped garden, repaired clothing and ran messages around the neighborhood.

Today, the board was mainly talking about the negotiations with the nearby farmers. Deals had been struck, but now only one farm was guaranteeing there would be food to be shared for the winter. They had said they would need more people to help when they slaughtered and prepared a few of the animals. Already, half the neighborhood was helping one farm with weeding and chores on Tuesdays and the other half was helping a different farm on Saturdays.

"They have to give us something for our work," Mr. Rodriguez said. "I know they have a well-stocked cellar. I had to carry some heavy pots up from there for the farmer's wife."

"They didn't say they wouldn't give us something, but their crop isn't looking great and they were going to share the beans and corn with us. They can't get fertilizer or weed killer," Mrs. Allen explained.

"They were going to think over what they could give us in exchange for our time. I should know more by next meeting."

"They better have something. I'm tired of eating pea soup every night."

Amber's dad did bring up the idea of dropping the sanitation checks and they all agreed it was not working out as well as they thought it might. It wasn't worth the arguments people were having over it, he had said.

"Hey guys, I have great news," Amber said as she plopped down on the couch in Alex's basement on Friday night. The four neighborhood teens had started to get together on Friday nights after the flyer had been found. The adults had encouraged them to do it so they could "still be kids." The adults knew they still needed some time to hang out and blow off steam after working so hard each day, so they were all encouraged to spend a night each week "having fun." Sometimes one of them would talk them through a movie. Sometimes, Alex brought his guitar and they had an impromptu dance or just sang along to their favorites. They did everything they could not to talk too much about their present situation.

"The power's coming back on tomorrow?" Shelley asked with a sarcastic tone to her voice.

"No, but there might be a bacon cheeseburger in our future," she replied.

"A what?" Alex said. "Oh, that would be awesome. How?"

"Well, it might just be a bacon hamburger wrapped in a

lettuce leaf since we have no cheese," she said. "They discussed helping the farmers slaughter some animals soon at the weekly meeting. We would then get a portion of the meat."

"Ugh. That's not something I could do," Susanna said. "I couldn't even dissect a worm for biology. I pretended to be sick that day."

"I'm sure I could do it if I had to," Alex said. "Were there enough adults to help, though?"

"The adults have it covered," Amber replied. "They didn't even bring up asking us to help."

"That's a first for them to overlook the teenage help," Shelley said. "I feel like I'm working three full-time jobs. I'd rather be in school. I'd even rather have Mr. Schnurr teach me all day long."

"Wow," Susanna said. "He's the worst, most boring teacher ever. And he blows his nose every other minute."

"Into a handkerchief, too!" Shelley said. "Then he stuffs it into his pocket. I don't think he even washes his hands."

They laughed and then Alex played some of the songs he knew. They all ended up going home earlier than they usually did. They were fighting to stay awake.

It was a Sunday when the first airplane flew over the neighborhood – July 21 for Ivy and July 23 for Veronica. The closest church was a 20-minute drive and no one wanted to walk hours to a church not knowing if there would be a service or not, especially not knowing for sure the date or what time a service might be. A church service was going on in the Jensen's house because they had a piano and hymnal. Most of the neighborhood gathered each Sunday to sing some hymns. Some of the men took turns giving a sermon. There were two Catholic families who had their own service down the street at the Reeds' home. The rest of the neighborhood enjoyed some quiet time on Sunday mornings. There was a basic routine to their new life. The entire neighborhood worked hard the rest of the time, but everyone knew a break was necessary for sanity. The only ones working on Sunday mornings were the two people on patrol for security.

Amber and her family had started going to church weekly after the flyer was found. They were all in the middle of saying the Lord's Prayer when the sound of the plane engine was recognized. Everyone stopped praying and ran outside. Their eyes followed the plane as it flew directly overhead and they saw it drop some big crates about 300 yards past the neighborhood in the woods across the street. The crowd all started heading toward the drop site and then mothers with children started lagging behind and stopping at the neighborhood entrance.

"We can't all go," Amber heard her father say as he stopped and turned to the crowd. They were on the edge of the small wooded area that separated their neighborhood from the farm to the south. There was a small creek that ran through the trees where a lot of families got water from every day. "Really, we can't all go! Let's be smart about this. We don't know what is in the crates. How about just five or six adults to check it out first?"

"I'll go," Mr. Thompson said quickly and three other men stepped forward, too. As soon as they were out of sight, Alex started following behind them. He disappeared before Amber could call after him.

The crowd stared after them and was silent for a full two seconds before they all started talking at once. The noise got louder as everyone else from the neighborhood started to gather.

Amber found a tree nearby that she could climb and started up, hoping to see where her father went but she couldn't see through all the branches and leaves in front of her.

As Amber climbed down, she heard someone running back from the woods. As soon as he broke out of the trees, Alex started talking.

"Lots of food … some supplies … bring wagons … quick!" He was gasping between bursts of words and he beckoned people to follow him quickly. A few people ran back to their houses, probably to get wagons, and the rest surged forward, racing toward food.

And then there was a gunshot. Everyone froze. It was silent. Amber had barely gotten down from the tree at that point and she hid behind the trunk.

"Alex, where are you? Tell them to bring the wagons – hurry!" Amber heard her dad's voice yell. "We're okay. It's safe."

A few of the men started running ahead to see what had happened and the rest of the crowd moved forward a little more cautiously. Amber ran – she had to see her dad.

"He pointed it right at me," Mr. Thompson was repeating over and over when Amber got to the crates. There was a solitary man lying facedown about thirty feet to the side of the crates. Dad came up beside Mr. Thompson and touched his arm. Amber was frozen in place but she kept her eyes on her dad, trying to ignore the body.

"He just came up and said that it was all his and pointed his gun at me," Mr. Thompson told her dad. "I had to shoot back. Looks like he was alone, though. Maybe he was hiding out at one of the local farms. I don't recognize him from any of our negotiation talks."

Jack patted him on the arm and moved him away from the man. He then looked up at the crowd. "We need to move these boxes fast. Now anyone in hearing distance knows there was a plane and a gunshot," he said. "Load up and move them to the playground. We'll inventory them there."

Amber's dad came over to her and she collapsed into him. He gave her a big hug and he picked her up for a second. Her heart seemed to be pounding in her chest.

"I'm okay, honey. You should have stayed with the kids. Get back there fast – I'll be right behind you."

Amber took one look at dad's face as he put her down and then took off running back to the neighborhood. There was sadness in his eyes. She glanced back once to see the boxes being loaded onto the wagons and the armed men keeping watch. She could feel some tears smarting in her eyes. Someone just died, she thought. She now lived in a world where people were going to fight over food. How bad would it get? she wondered. She was glad she hadn't seen the man's face. She could almost pretend she hadn't seen a dead body. Almost. She found her mom and her brother at the playground and gave her mom a hug. Mom hugged her back fiercely and Amber felt the tears slide down her cheeks. It wasn't until they stopped that she let go of her mom. When she looked up at her, she could tell her mom had guessed what had happened. They didn't talk, but just held hands and watched the activity at the playground.

Once all the boxes from the crates were at the playground, Amber's dad faced the crowd. Amber could sense the eagerness in everyone to see what the boxes contained. Everyone was hungry. She pictured them all fighting over the food. If that happened, someone would get hurt.

"The crates had 'More coming' and '3 month rations' painted on them. I promise this is all of the boxes and we will go through them and distribute them fairly among all our families. One man threatened us and we protected ourselves. Let's have the HOA board come up and help with inventory and then heads of families can meet back here by late afternoon to pick up their share. Or you can stay and watch," Jack said.

Amber stayed to watch. Alex was soon by her side and they whispered back and forth about what they saw in the boxes. When Amber's mind would wander back to seeing the dead man, she'd focus on counting what was coming out of the boxes. Two of the boxes were full of vitamins, basic medical supplies and batteries, which would be great for their flashlights. They tried to rely on natural light as much as possible, using their candles and flashlights only when they were really needed. The other boxes were full of MREs – meals ready to eat. They were full of calories and could feed two people for a day under emergency conditions. Amber's dad often bought them for his camping trips and brought extras home. She knew the military used them a lot. There had been twelve boxes in each crate.

They were lucky enough to have had enough food by then from everyone's pantries and gardens. There had also been some successful hunting, although no one went to bed feeling full. Deer were plentiful in the area, but they were careful to only take one or two at a time since they had to use the meat right away. The day of the airdrop, everyone got a full MRE and finally went to bed with a full stomach again.

"What happened to the guy that got shot?" Christopher asked their dad after dinner that night. He was tapping his foot like crazy, which was always a sign that something was bothering him, but he wasn't crying. He had a lot more responsibility now than a nine-year-old was supposed to have.

"A few guys went back and buried him. He didn't have any identification, but they marked the spot in case someone comes looking for him," her dad said.

"It's just so sad," her mom said. "There was plenty to go around. He could have just asked. We would have shared."

"People do drastic things when they're hungry," he replied.

Even though it was warm in her bedroom, she liked having her privacy at the end of the day so she chose to sleep there instead of in the living room with the rest of her family. They usually had a nice breeze with the screen door opened. She kept the window open at night and the room seemed to cool down a bit as soon as the sun set. Amber tried really hard to block out seeing the man as she tried to fall asleep, but just couldn't get the picture out of her head. She ended up crying herself to sleep instead. She hoped the man hadn't left behind a family and that they weren't waiting on him to bring home food.

CHAPTER SIX

Amber welcomed the weather turning cooler as fall approached. She felt like she was sweating all day and all night that summer. She was usually outside helping weed their garden or the farmers' fields or inside doing clothing repair. The only time she felt cool that summer was when it was raining.

The worst part to her, though, was that they were down to weekly baths, and it wasn't even really a bath. They were allowed to warm up a pan of water over the fire pit after dinner and then take it to the bathroom and pretty much give themselves a sponge bath. Amber and most of the women had cut their hair pretty short by that point so there was less to wash. Amber barely had enough water to rinse the soap out of her hair after washing her body. Everyone in the neighborhood smelled, but no one ever commented on it.

When it did rain, many people in the neighborhood put on their swimsuits and took a "nature shower," as her mom liked to call it. With a bar of soap, they could get really clean as long as it wasn't a thunderstorm. It had rained all day before the weekly meeting, so when they had to meet inside because of the wind, at least everyone smelled better than normal.

"I have some bad news," Jack said once they called the weekly meeting to order. "Mr. Allen and I visited the three nearby farms yesterday to get an update on the help they want for harvest time.

"The Turners and the Westerlys have decided they no longer need our help. Their crop is turning out to be much smaller than they expected and they don't have enough to share."

"But, we've been weeding for them all summer and doing patrols of their farms!" Mr. Rodriquez interrupted.

"I mentioned that to them," Jack said. Amber saw him make eye contact with Mr. Allen before he continued. "Most of their family members are going to head to the malls for the winter so the Turners offered to designate two of their cows for us to slaughter when we need meat and any extra eggs they have that their chickens lay. The Westerlys offered a pig, eggs and any extra milk they have since one of their cows is due to give birth soon. They both said if we need to, we could also kill a few chickens, but to leave enough for laying eggs."

Amber saw Mr. Rodriquez relax in his seat. Most of the adults in the room were nodding their heads. Amber had learned from the farmers that eggs didn't need to be refrigerated until they were cleaned off, so they could sit in a basket for days in a shady spot before they needed to be used. She had heard her dad talk about using salt from one of the famers to salt the meat to keep it longer or building a smokehouse in their neighborhood.

"The board is accepting their offers," Mrs. Allen said. "The Speers do want help with harvest, though. It will take a good chunk of our people helping them for several days to harvest all the corn and beans."

Amber liked the Speers. She had been over to help Mrs. Speer mend clothes several times. Mrs. Speer enjoyed sewing with a machine, but her hands hurt when she sewed by hand. Her children were away at college in Nebraska and Alabama and they usually had family come to help with the harvest, as Mr. Speer's uncle owned his own equipment. Mrs. Speer had told Amber they had planned this year to be their last harvest. They were going to put their farm on the market in the spring but now they were stuck until the power came back on. No one was going to buy a farm when you had to do everything by hand.

"Plans always seem to change, though," she said. "We

were hoping to sell when they were building all the houses, too. Farming isn't what it used to be."

Amber had patted Mrs. Speer's arm and then had gone back to fixing up a hole in Mr. Speer's coat. She hoped Mrs. Speer's sons were trying to make their way back home, but traveling anywhere was so hard now. Mrs. Speer just seemed sad most of the time; she only smiled when her husband was near or when Amber showed her a finished mending project, assuring Amber it was as good as if she had done it herself.

With the farm resources and the July airdrop, it looked like the neighborhood and the Speers would have just enough food to get through until the spring. However, Amber noticed that almost everyone she encountered anymore tended to look up to the sky a lot more often than they used to do. At every weekly meeting, someone would mention how great it would be to get another food drop soon. There were none all fall, though.

"Snow!" Christopher yelled, waking Amber up one morning. She could feel the cold before she opened her eyes. It had been a nice fall day the day before, but now her nose and the arm outside the covers were chilly. She sat up and looked out her window to see a slight dusting of snow and then cuddled up under her blankets to get warm. A few minutes later, she heard an airplane. She ran downstairs to where the rest of her family were standing at the opened front door in their pajamas.

They watched as the plane flew across sky, leaving behind a trail of papers. Dad left to go to his bedroom and came back a few minutes later with boots, a coat, a hat and gloves on.

"I'll go see what it says," he said. "Close the door and stay warm."

Amber went back to her room and put on three layers of clothing and took her blankets down to the couch. Christopher was there already with his blankets and they actually sat close together without saying anything to get warm. It wasn't long before their mom joined them.

They heard Dad come back in, but no one got up from the couch. They waited for him to come to them. He found them and got under the blankets and handed Mom the flyer.

"It's basically the same one as before," she said. "It just has some helpful tips on the back that we already know about."

"I know," he sighed. "We can go out later and collect the papers for the fires."

"How are we going to do all the things we have to do with it being so cold?" Christopher asked. "Can I just stay home?"

"You'll just have to bundle up," Dad said. "We will really need to check all the gardens before anyone does anything else today. I'll check with Ivy and Veronica, but I'm guessing most things need to get harvested today in case the cold stays."

"I can go talk to them," Mom said. "Amber, you come with me to check on their clothes. We need to make sure they have enough blankets, too."

"When you come back, I'll talk to Mrs. Allen about the harvest and then we can split up to let everyone know," he said. "At least we're all in this together."

I hope it's a short winter, Amber thought. She never liked being cold.

A week later, they heard another airplane when it was almost dusk. This time, the drop was close by in the Speers' farmland. It was identical to the first drop. Amber and Christopher split the chilimac MRE that night and Amber was so thankful to feel full. There had even been a brownie to split. That was the last night she slept in her room for a while. The weather turned bitterly cold the next day and their parents decided it would be best if they all slept together in their bed and piled all the blankets in the house on top. It was their best chance at all being warm while they slept.

They spent more time inside during the winter months. Without gardens, patrol duty was just during the day so no one needed to be outside at night when it was coldest. They didn't think they would get many people just walking down the road during the cold weather. Water still needed to be collected daily, but Amber hoped many families had found buckets like hers did to collect snow and bring them inside to thaw. They were also using a bucket in the bathroom like a chamber pot and they took turns emptying it in their outhouse. Amber's family had a continual game of Monopoly going on, although sometimes Miss Gray jumped up and rearranged all the pieces, usually when Amber was winning.

One day when the wind was howling against their house, there was a knock at their door. Dad jumped up to get it and found Mrs. Allen and Nancy Gillespie at the door.

Nancy was a nurse and had lived in her home with her fiancé, David. David had broken off the engagement the month before that fateful Easter and never contacted Nancy again. She was going to sell the house and go to medical school, but became the neighborhood nurse when the power went out. She was learning all she could about herbalism from books she found at the Thompsons' house. Amber was often sent to get her advice on an ailment for families in the neighborhood.

Dad brought them in quickly and they started whispering to him in the hallway. Amber could see them from the edge of the couch where they had all been sitting with several blankets while Mom read *Treasure Island* out loud. Mrs. Allen had her arm around Nancy and it looked like Nancy was crying. Dad reached out and put an arm on each of them. He said something very quietly and then the women opened the door and left. It couldn't be good news, Amber thought. He returned to the couch and sat back between Mom and Christopher. They waited for him to talk.

"The Rodriquez baby passed away this morning," he said quietly.

"No!" Her mom said and started crying. Dad put his arm around her. The baby had been born just a few weeks before Easter.

"What happened?" Amber asked, her voice cracking. She could feel her own tears forming.

"Nancy said the baby started coughing two days ago and

it just kept getting worse. When Mrs. Rodriquez woke up this morning …" Her dad couldn't finish. Even Christopher was crying at this news. They all sat on the couch, doing their best to grieve and console each other until their stomachs said it was time for lunch. Amber decided to try and nap after lunch. Christopher joined her. As she was about to head upstairs, she heard her dad say he would head over there in a few days to help bury the baby.

"I never thought we'd live in a world like this," her mom said.

"I don't think anyone did," Amber said to herself and then walked up the stairs.

Amber didn't expect much to happen at all to mark her sixteenth birthday. Yet, on what the neighborhood deemed to be December 8, there was a candy bar by her plate at dinner.

"Where did you find this?" Amber asked her parents.

"I found it in our basement in a box of granola," Alex said. His family had joined hers for dinner that night to celebrate. "My mom had forgotten about her secret stash. We decided to keep them hidden for special occasions. There's still five left! I can't wait until my birthday next month."

Amber laughed. Everyone seemed happy for a while that night. She shared her candy bar with her brother and Alex. Both sets of parents declined even a tiny bite. She caught her parents glancing at her a few times that night with a strange look on their faces. She guessed what they were thinking, though. It was a strange and different world than either of them had expected to be living in when their child turned sixteen. It was supposed to be a big celebration with a dinner out, friends over for a sleepover and getting a driver's license. Now, it was a small gathering with a candy bar and work tomorrow. Like most days, she was just glad her family was together and could lean on each other to get through these times. Poor Mike still didn't know where his parents were.

After Alex's family left, Amber thanked her parents for the great birthday.

"Sorry we couldn't do what we normally do," her dad

said. "Barbecue Bill's would have tasted really good tonight."

"We had planned to get you a top-of-the-line sewing machine this year and some more classes with Trina," her mom said. "Although, you've probably learned more just by doing the repairs you've done these last few months."

"It's okay. I had a great time tonight," Amber said. "Someday, the power will be back on and you can make it up to me. By then, I'll probably just want a car." They all laughed at that.

A week before the snow melted away, Nancy came to their door again in the middle of the day. This time, her dad wasn't there. He was doing patrol duty that day. However, Nancy asked her mom to pass along a message. Mrs. Tenny had passed away in her sleep the night before. Nancy and her mom looked sad, but there weren't tears like before. Mrs. Tenny had been living alone for a while. Her husband passed away suddenly a few months after they moved into their house two years ago. Amber didn't know her very well.

At the weekly meeting the next day, several of the adults got into an argument about whether the people who dug up the grave would get extra food rations for the extra work. Her father had argued against it, saying they had to make sure there was enough food for the children until we got food from the gardens again. He was overruled by one vote. Amber thought her father had a good point, but then there was another airdrop of food that afternoon and the thought of being hungry wasn't a problem anymore, or at least for a while.

CHAPTER SEVEN

As soon as all the snow had melted away in the spring, Amber stayed outside as much as possible. The entire neighborhood seemed to have the same idea. Amber was mending some shirts on her front porch when she saw some adults start to gather at the neighborhood entrance.

"They're back!" she heard someone shout. The group started heading toward the playground area and Amber saw her dad was there. She knew he had patrol duty that day. Is that the Sanders? she wondered. She put the shirts back in the house quickly and headed to the playground area.

"They arrested him," she heard Mrs. Sanders say to Jack. Her son, Ben, was holding her hand but had some grocery bags in the other hand. "We don't know where they took him."

The Jacksons were with them, too, and they were carrying a few grocery bags each.

"Where are the Polks?" her dad asked. Mr. Jackson spoke up.

"They were taken to a different facility the day after we got to the mall," he said. "Families with young children were taken to a military base. They said it would be safer for the children there."

"The food was starting to run low at the mall," Mrs. Sanders said. "Derrick said we should come home. We'd be better off here. Then, he said we'd need food for the trip home ..." She started crying. Ben let go of her hand, dropped the grocery bags and took off toward the playground equipment where Mike was playing.

"The military security came up to us shortly after that with a few bags of MREs and told us we had to leave," Mrs. Jackson said as she put her hand on Mrs. Sanders' shoulder. "They had arrested Mr. Sanders for stealing food and we were not welcome to come back."

"Why don't you guys come to our house and we can talk more about what happened there and here while you were gone," Jack said. Mrs. Allen followed them to the house.

"What was that all about?" Alex asked her. He had just come out of his house as the adults were walking toward her house. Amber caught him up on what she had heard.

"Well, at least we'll have one more person for patrols now," Alex said.

"Yes, but that's now four more people to feed," Amber said. "I heard my dad say he was going to check with Ivy and Veronica about how early we could start planting."

"I never appreciated veggies before all this," Alex said. "Some fresh green beans sound wonderful after a winter of MREs."

"I agree," Amber said, "but, MREs sometimes have chocolate."

"You got me there!"

Two days later at the next neighborhood meeting, they added the Jacksons and Mrs. Sanders to the work rotations. Mrs. Sanders and Ben decided to live in the Clarks' house with Mike and his grandma so Mrs. Sanders could help take care of Mike. Then, they discussed the food situation in-depth. Without another drop soon, they would need to start hunting again. They were going to encourage everyone to expand their backyard garden plots but both Ivy and Veronica had agreed that they couldn't safely plant anything outside until early May. However, they were personally going to start seedlings in their houses to try and get an earlier crop going.

The teens had just gotten settled in Alex's backyard the next Friday night when they heard Alex's dad shouting from the front of Amber's house.

"Mark's gone missing! Jack, we need to get everyone out to go look for him!"

Amber's first thought was that Mark was Austin and Ella's dad. They would be so upset if something happened to their father. She jumped up and ran to the front of the house. The others followed. Amber's parents were in their yard and Alex's mom was running toward them.

"What do you mean missing?" Jack asked Mr. McCarthy.

"We were staying together like we're supposed to but then a few hours ago, we spotted a deer running. Mark took off after it even though I told him we wouldn't get it if we ran. I picked up our backpacks and then tried to catch up with him, but by then I couldn't see him. It was dusk, but I should have been able to see him. I looked and looked and called for him, but …"

"How far away were you guys?" Jack asked.

"About fifteen minutes north of here," he replied. "We can get some flashlights and get there before …"

"Brian, I think we need to wait until tomorrow. We just can't see much in the dark, even with flashlights."

Mr. McCarthy looked at Jack and then at his wife. She nodded her head and his whole body shrugged in dejection.

"Justine, take him home," Jack said. "It's not your fault, Brian. Sherrie, let's go talk to Mrs. Allen."

Alex followed his parents into his house and Shelley and Susanna headed back to their houses. Amber went inside and found Christopher staring at nothing in the living room. She just sat down beside him and put an arm around him. They stayed like that until her parents came home.

"Did they find him?" Christopher asked. "Austin is going to be worried."

"No," Mom said. "They're going to do a search party at first light."

Amber tossed and turned a lot that night in her own room. First Mr. Sanders had been arrested and now Mr. Allen was missing. She thought about the baby who died and Mrs. Tenny passing away. A year ago, she spent most of her time thinking about clothing design. Today, life felt a lot more dangerous and less secure. Even Christopher was acting differently. He tended to sleep near their parents, but tonight he had insisted he was going to sleep in his own room from now on. And, he didn't want to talk about it, he said.

More than half of the neighborhood spent all morning the next day scouring the area where Mr. McCarthy said he last saw Mark Allen. They didn't find anything. When they got home, Mike's grandma told them the Speers had stopped by to report a drop of food near their house. For the next two weeks, Mrs. Allen and Mr. McCarthy would go out for an hour or two at the end of each day and search, but they found no traces of Mr. Allen. After those two weeks, Mrs. Allen made an announcement at the weekly meeting.

"I want to thank everyone who helped look for my husband," she said as she teared up. "I know he would never have left us and I now have to assume the worst. My kids and I will have to rely on you all more for help now."

The room was quiet as Mrs. Allen started crying. Amber's dad spoke up to take the attention off her.

"Mark was a great friend. When you are ready, we can have a memorial service for him if you'd like." Several people nodded their heads and Amber noticed a few women trying to slyly dab their eyes with fingers.

On one unseasonably warm night a few weeks later, Amber's father wanted to have an extended meeting with all the adults in the neighborhood to do a new inventory and he asked if she would watch all the children at the playground with the other teens while the adults met in their backyard. However, it started to rain and got very windy, so her father took the adults to their basement and the children were taken next door to Alex's basement. Amber knew the basement was unfinished, so she found some chalk and books to help keep the children entertained. While the other teens hung out on the stairs, shined the flashlights and took children to the bathroom, Amber started reading stories out loud to any children who would sit and listen. The rest of the children either ran around or used the chalk to draw on the ground. Eventually, the crowd of children at her feet grew bigger and bigger and she started asking questions at the end of each story.

"I miss school," said Alison at the end of *Horton Hears a Who*.

"Really?" Amber said. "What do you miss about it?"

"Well, I only know some of my ABCs and can only read a few baby books. My sisters were both reading when they were 6 – they tell me that all the time!"

"I could teach you how to read," Amber said.

"Really?" the girl said with wide, blue eyes. "My parents and sisters have been too busy."

Amber read a few more stories, but the children were getting restless and needed to move around. Alex had some of the boys working with some wood and nails to build a stool. She drew some hopscotch squares on the floor for the girls and then took Alison aside with some chalk. She went through the alphabet and saw that the girl knew just about all of them. She then told her each letter had one or two sounds. Once you knew the sounds, you could put them together and figure out what a word was. She started with the little girl's name.

"Meeting's over!" shouted one of the other teens as parents started to come downstairs.

Amber told her father that night what she had done during the meeting and suggested they start a neighborhood school.

"That is a terrific idea! Do you want to be the teacher?"

"Could I? That would be great!"

Amber spent the next few days looking at the different books people had at their houses and coming up with a plan in her free time. The next week, school was in session for four hours for two days a week in Trebein Trails.

CHAPTER EIGHT

When the weather got warm enough that Amber didn't need to wear a jacket anymore, she started hearing two to three airplanes fly over every week – mostly military aircraft. It was almost June, according to Ivy and Veronica. Amber stopped looking up at the sound anymore unless the plane sounded really loud or low.

"Government first, people second," Amber would hear the adults say when a fighter plane flew overhead. She tended to look up for those since they were loud.

Her parents had guessed the government would need to fix up the military planes and trucks first so they could be used to deliver supplies. They were hoping power would be restored before they went through another winter, but then a plane dropped another round of flyers and those hopes were quickly dashed.

My fellow Americans,

We have been able to re-establish a basic military structure to start delivering supplies to locations throughout the country and to provide a basic level of defense. We brought back almost all of our equipment that was overseas since they were still operational. Food pallets are being dropped at strategic places throughout the country. Please share with your neighbors. Trucks will soon appear in two waves. The first wave will assess the damages and needs of each area and the second wave will start doing repair work. We will work from the coastlines inward and focus more airdrops in the

Midwest while they wait. The more we get repaired, the faster we will work. When the trucks come, they will ask for volunteers to work on the repair efforts. Compensations will come in credits toward new appliances, electronic parts and vehicles as they become available. Be assured that help will come. Please carefully read the instructions on the back regarding sanitation, proper burial practices, ways to find food, how to purify water and basic first aid.

It, too, was signed by the President.

The back was full of tips for the new no-electricity lifestyle; however, there was nothing Amber didn't already know now.

"When do you think they'll come, Dad?" Amber asked that night at dinner. Dinner was a simple stew of carrots, kale and a small amount of deer meat that their mom had cooked over the fire pit.

Her father stared out their back window and sighed.

"I honestly don't know, Amber," he said. "I hope we only have to face one more winter. This lifestyle is tiring."

He turned back to face his family and forced a smile. "We didn't know how good we had it, did we?"

"I don't know what I would do in a grocery store anymore," her mom said. "To have choices … I think I miss the refrigerator most, though."

"I miss ice cream," Amber said. "And, long, hot showers."

"What about cell phones?" her brother asked. "I miss calling Uncle Donny on Sundays. He always had a new joke for me."

They all went silent. Uncle Donny was their mom's brother. He was a high school math teacher and baseball coach in Orlando.

"I'm sure he's okay," Mom said. "He was always very resourceful. At least the weather should be nice in Florida."

"One more winter," Dad said. "I'm sure that's all we'll have to go through. Let's start figuring out how we can do that and focus on the here and now."

Her father never liked to think about the past or even a future with power. The problem was right in front of him and he didn't want to waste time on maybes.

As Amber headed to teach school the next morning, she saw Susanna walking really slowly up the street.

"Susanna, why are you limping?" Amber asked her as she ran to catch up with her. No one had dared called her anything but her full name ever since she beat up some boy at school in the fifth grade for calling her "Suzy." Susanna was two years older than Amber, yet Amber had heard about that fight right after it happened. Word had traveled fast at Lincoln Elementary. Once Amber was alongside Susanna and looked at her face, she could see the girl was in serious pain. "Are you headed to Nurse Nancy's house? Do you need help?"

"Yes, but I can go myself," Susanna said and shrugged off Amber's arm. Amber stood still for a minute and watched Susanna head toward the nurse's house. She probably has a huge blister, Amber thought, and headed across the street to the "schoolhouse." They had decided to let her set up her classroom in the Polk's house since they were not expected to come home any time soon from the military base. They had left behind a lot of toys and craft supplies, along with children's books since they had a 5-year-old girl. They also had a swing set and slide in their backyard and Amber tried to have class out there when she could so the little kids could take play breaks.

A few days later, Amber's mom almost let her and Christopher start eating dinner before Amber's father got home. It was rare that they didn't wait until all four of them were home, but it was getting late. Just as they were sitting down, he came through the door and sat right down at the table.

"I'm sorry to do this before we eat, but I'm late because I heard some bad news," he took a moment and looked both Christopher and Amber in the eye and then took his wife's hand. "Susanna passed away this afternoon."

"What? I just saw her going to Nurse Nancy's a few days ago. She was limping, but very much alive! Are you sure?" Amber couldn't believe what she was hearing.

Her dad got up and kneeled by her side. He took her hand.

"She was limping because she cut her foot on an ax chopping wood a few weeks ago. She didn't want to bother anyone so she tried to take care of it herself. It got infected and spread in her blood. There was nothing Nancy could have done for her."

Amber pushed back from the table and ran up to her room. While tears were pricking her eyes, she was mostly angry with Susanna. She was old enough to know better, to know how dangerous their world had gotten. And why was that? Susanna should have been away at college anyway, not chopping wood. Amber should be worrying about grades and scholarships and creating fun outfits with a new sewing machine. Where were the trucks that were supposed to come and help them?

"Why does life have to be this way right now?" Amber whispered as she started sobbing into her pillow. She fell asleep quickly, exhausted with grief.

The Reeds decided to bury Susanna in their backyard a few days later. It was heartbreaking for Amber to watch Susanna's little sisters, Samantha and Alison, crying at the funeral. Amber held mom's hand during the whole service. She still felt mad most of the time, but she couldn't help but cry today. Only the necessary work was done in the neighborhood that day. Another family was given the two-week period of mourning. Amber cried herself to sleep most nights and was extra careful with everything she did during the day. She couldn't believe that she lived in a world where a small cut could lead to a teenager's death.

CHAPTER NINE

"Can we go to the museum today?" Alison asked after Amber closed *The Wind in the Willows*. They were reading outside. The weather had gotten more bearable now that summer was drawing to a close. Amber had a soft spot for the little girl, especially after her big sister, Susanna's, death. She had trouble telling her no. She was always well behaved and she would make an adorable face and look at her with her big, brown eyes when she asked for something she really wanted. Over the past three months, Amber had found one of the best ways to teach the kids was to read to them every day. It could cover vocabulary, history, science and social studies, depending on the story she chose.

The "museum" was a house at the entrance of the neighborhood. The couple that lived in the house had been gone on a house-hunting trip to Florida when the power went out. The trek back to North Carolina was probably out of the question for them since they still hadn't returned a year and a half later.

No one bothered with the house except to scavenge some supplies. One of the writing assignments she had the children do early on was to write about what they missed most about the power being on. They mostly talked about school friends and food, so Amber decided to ask if she could give them a tour of the abandoned house and show them all the appliances, too. Most of them remembered them, but a few of the younger ones seemed to have fading memories. She called it the "Museum Tour," and they asked to go on it again at least once a month. She thought it would be easier for them when the power came back on to remember what everything did. There were three televisions, a microwave, a refrigerator, various kitchen appliances, lamps, clock radios and even a computer in the office.

"Miss Amber, what did this do again?" Ella asked as she opened the refrigerator door. Ella was 7 now and always had a question, even though she usually knew the answer.

"It kept your food cold – don't you remember?" Austin scolded his younger sister gently.

"Why keep food cold? We don't do that now," Ella said. She knew the answers to her questions, but liked to press her brother's buttons.

"I remember," Samantha said. "There was so much food back then. After a meal, you could put anything leftover in the refrigerator and save it for later. The food wouldn't spoil if it was kept cold."

"That's right, Samantha," Amber said. Samantha liked to take on the role of her assistant since he was the oldest kid at the school. The few other older children in the neighborhood didn't come to school. There was too much work to do. It was sometimes hard for some of these little ones to spend the ten hours a week away from home, too. They just met two hours a day after lunch Monday through Friday. With no electricity, clothes had to be washed by hand, water had to be boiled for cooking and cleaning, fires had to be tended, bread had to be kneaded and baked, gardens had to be tended, the neighborhood border had to be patrolled, game had to be hunted, supplies had to be scavenged, clothes had to be mended and created by hand, they had to help the local farmer ... there was a never-ending list of things to do every day – and even the little ones had to pitch in.

"Samantha, why don't you be our tour guide today? Blake hasn't seen the museum yet," Amber said. Blake was 5 and his parents had just decided to let them come to school after Amber visited them. She knew the parents didn't expect much and treated it like babysitting, but she hoped she could teach him to read over the next few months.

She hung back a little and listened as Samantha showed them the oven and a coffeemaker in the kitchen.

"The coffeemaker even heated the water for you! My parents used to have the coffee ready and waiting for them when they woke up," she heard Samantha say.

Samantha then led them into the living room where the TV, two lamps and a computer were.

"You could type a message and someone on the other side of the world could read it within seconds." She was repeating the very same words Amber had used when she gave them the tour. They all nodded, but most remembered exactly what a computer was.

Then, she took them to the back hall where a washer and dryer sat. Ella stared at the washer and dryer every time they came. She was old enough to help her mom do laundry by hand. Her mother, Mrs. Allen, now did laundry for some of the older people in Trebein Trails as a way of pitching in for the neighborhood.

Amber caught up to the group as they approached the door to the garage. There were some cars in the neighborhood, but none of them worked. Most were at the end of people's driveways, moved out of the garage so there could be room for other things in the garage, such as beds when the weather was too warm for sleeping in the house. As the door opened, the children saw a red convertible, a motorcycle, a speedboat and a riding lawn mower.

"Wow," Blake said. "That looks like my Hot Wheels car – in real life!" He said that every time they came, but this time he pulled it out of his pocket to show the other kids.

"People used to travel far and wide in cars and even on things like that over there – it's called a motorcycle," Amber said. "Imagine being able to travel 500 miles in one day."

"Do you think we'll ever be able to do that again?" Ella asked.

"I know you will," Amber answered. "You live in America and if there is one place in the world that won't stop until we get the power back on, it's here. In fact, that leads in to what we'll be studying next in history – American inventors. I found a book in Mrs. Thompson's library that we can use. All sorts of important things were invented right here in this country. But, that's enough for today. I'll see you all on Thursday. Samantha, can you make sure they all get home? I need to close up the doors here."

"Sure, Ms. Amber."

The class left and she watched them out the front door. She closed her eyes and listened to their laughter and sing-song voices. For a moment, she could take herself back to the "normal" world when she was their age. Life was so easy then and there was no way they could have known how blessed they were. Then she heard a humming sound that kept getting louder. She quickly opened her eyes and stepped outside. The children were running back to her.

"Ms. Amber! Ms. Amber! It's a truck!"

"Quickly – get in the house!"

She got them all in the house and closed the door right as the truck came around the corner from the entrance to the subdivision. She went to the kitchen and peeked out the window there, telling the children to stay down.

It was a large, military truck painted green and black with two men inside and four men in the bed. The men in the bed each had a rifle. They came to a stop just inside the neighborhood and the two men in the truck got out. They also had rifles. They all looked up and Amber wondered what they were looking at. Then, the four from the bed of the truck started walking back to the entrance, with two stopping at the bend in the road. She heard another truck coming – big and bulky and white, with a lift bucket on it. The white truck parked right in front of the "museum" house and three men got out.

"Yep, these poles look good," one said. "We just need to re-run the wire."

One word ran through Amber's head and she said it out loud, "Power."

Amber waited until her father showed up before stepping out of the "museum" house. She had told the children to hide in one of the bedrooms. She waited on the porch until she could catch her father's eye. He was talking to the two military men and when they pointed toward the power lines at the entrance to the neighborhood, he saw her and waved her over.

She motioned that she wanted to whisper something to him and told him about the children in the house and asked what she should do.

"It's okay, Amber," he said. "These men are here to help. Tell the children to head home for the day and have them tell their parents that there will be a meeting tonight."

She went back to the house and did what he had told her to do. Meetings were commonplace now – everyone knew they were held at the playground during good weather and at their house during inclement weather with the children next door at Alex's house. They were always held about an hour before dusk and when the world got dark, the meeting was over. There were also messengers to pass along any information and Amber was one of those. She left her father and started going to houses without school children to tell them about the meeting.

Alex caught up with her by the third house, out of breath from running.

"Is it true? Are they here to turn the power back on?" he asked.

"How do you know so fast? Aren't you on patrol today?"

"I just got off duty and Shelley told me there was a power truck. I ran back as fast as I could to find out what was going on. Do you know? Is it true?"

"I don't know much. I'm spreading the word about tonight's meeting. My dad's talking with the guys. I saw them drive up when I was giving the kids a tour of the 'museum' house. It's a power truck and a military truck. Could they just turn the power back on?"

"I hope so," Alex said. "Back to normal life ..."

"What's normal anymore?" she asked. "I don't think the stores are automatically going to be full or that cars are just going to work again."

Alex wasn't listening to her. She could tell he was imaging life with electricity again, murmuring about video games and ice cream. After more than a year without power, she had grown used to their new lifestyle and had stopped missing some of the electronic distractions they used to have. She enjoyed the connections she had with people whom she'd had long conversations with; although, she would love to have ice cream again.

At the meeting that night, everyone was talking about the power coming back on, as any bit of news traveled fast in the neighborhood. Amber's father had to call the meeting to order by blowing on his whistle.

"Today, we had two trucks enter our neighborhood. They are from the government and they are here to help – really," he said.

Many adults laughed, but Amber didn't understand why. She would ask her father about that later.

"However, they can't just turn the power back on. The government has repaired all the main power grids and telephone lines, but almost anything electronic was fried during the solar flare and needs to be repaired or replaced. That includes the transformer that brings power to us and the circuit breaker boxes in our houses. These men are here to do the preliminary scouting work. Let me let them tell you what they are here to do."

"Thanks, Mr. Birch," said a man in military fatigues. "I'm Captain Casey Roberts and we are here to help. However, we are not here to turn the power on – yet, but …"

The neighborhood started shouting at questions, "Why not?" "It's been over a year – how much longer?" "Did you bring food?"

"But …" Capt. Roberts said in a loud, commanding voice that quieted the crowd. "… the next truck that comes will be here to turn on the power. We are here to get details on exactly what your neighborhood needs to re-establish power. We will get the list back to our headquarters and they will send out a repair and supply truck. This usually takes no more than three months; however, sometimes it can take longer during wintertime. My guess is that you should have power back on by the spring at the latest. We will re-establish power to each house by replacing the transformer and all circuit breakers. We will also show you how to repair a refrigerator and leave you parts to complete repairs. Telephones will also be furnished and you will be given a list of numbers to help with any repair questions or news updates. The rest of the electronic supplies and parts, along with vehicles, can be purchased as they become available. Currency and barter will be considered and the exchange rate will be given to you as each item becomes available.

"Now, I know that feels like a long time, but they will also be sending an airdrop of food and supplies as soon as headquarters gets the inventory list, which includes how many people you have here. It should be enough to get you through winter. We will also leave you with a pallet of food and some first aid supplies. We will also install one phone line while we're here.

"There is also an opportunity for more food and supplies. We need more workers to help go out on repair missions and work at the headquarters helping do inventory, load trucks and work in the phone center answering calls. For each person from your neighborhood that volunteers to work, your food drop will be increased by ten percent. Those who volunteer will be fed three meals a day, have a bed to sleep in a climate-controlled building, and will earn credits for their family to be used for buying electronics, parts and vehicles when they become available.

"We will stay at the entrance of your neighborhood until shortly after sunrise the day after tomorrow and then we must move on to the next neighborhood. Let us know before then if you want to volunteer to work and bring your birth certificate. Volunteers have to be 16 years old or older. Also, please stay in your homes tomorrow morning until we come by. We have to visually verify each person and we can only re-establish power to houses that are currently lived in. Thank you for your cooperation. Any questions?"

The crowd surged forward to ask him questions, but Amber turned to Alex.

"Want to go?"

"Yes! Do you think our parents will let us?"

"I'm not sure, but we're both 16, so we might be considered close to adults in this new world. We both already do adult work now."

"I don't think they can let too many of us go since there's so much to do here every day, but it would be great to get away for a while."

"And, they don't have long until the power comes back on."

"Let's do it!"

"Okay!"

The government workers had also brought a stack of newspapers with them and everyone poured over every word. Amber had to wait a while before she could look at a copy and then she shared with Alex. The death count was staggering, especially in major cities. Canada and Mexico had only lost power close to the U.S. border, so they started offering help right away. The first planes used for supply drops were from Canada.

"I don't know if we need the television or Internet anymore," Alex's mom, Justine, had said to Sherrie. "It's been nice to have a quiet life and talk with neighbors."

The workers got out a box of car parts and several of the men were already working on getting a car started again.

"Are stores open? Any gas stations working? What will we find if we leave the neighborhood?" were the main questions the crowd asked.

At this point, the workers said that the country was about a third of the way restored with basic power. The main problem lay with transportation. They had to go out to each neighborhood and house since people couldn't come to get the repair equipment and supplies. At first, they followed train lines with steam engines and used airplanes. Then, they got enough trucks up and running. Supply planes and boats were coming from other countries and while some were donations, others were from countries that were keeping track of each item they were sending. Slowly, cars and gas stations were getting repaired and some small stores were being established near big neighborhoods. There was more bartering going on than using real money.

Amber went to her room when she got home later that day instead of helping with dinner. She sat on her bed and looked around her room. Miss Gray hopped up beside her and Amber picked her up and cuddled her. Should she go away and work? What could happen in a year? Should she stay since the power was going to come back on soon? She knew she was helpful in the neighborhood with teaching the kids, sewing and running errands. If she left, though, she could be a part of helping the entire country rebuild. If her teenage years weren't going to be anywhere near normal, she might as well make them mean something big, she thought.

When she went down for dinner when she was called, her family all were smiling and seemed happier than they'd been in a long time.

"A hot shower is just going to be glorious," Mom said.

"I'm going to watch every movie we own for days on end," Christopher declared.

"You're probably going to have to go back to school soon, too," Dad reminded him. Christopher frowned. "Well, maybe not for a while."

"Alex and I were thinking of going and helping at the government place," Amber finally said, looking down. She gripped her hands in her lap and finally looked up at her mom. She was staring at her, eyes wide.

"You want to leave?" her mom asked. "Why?"

"I think it would be good for me to do something to help everyone," she said. "And, it would earn our family credits for a car, air conditioner parts, furnace parts, and maybe even a washing machine. Can you imagine having a working washing machine again?"

"Who would teach the children?" her dad asked.

"I will miss teaching them, but most of them are doing just fine," Amber said. "I thought I could leave a reading list and they could just work on book reports. I'm sure once the power is on, schools will start operating again soon, too. I doubt most neighborhoods had 'school,' so I bet our kids are even farther ahead than most their age."

"Do you think it'll be safe for you?" her mother asked.

"Alex wants to go, too, and we'll stick together. We're

both almost 17."

She caught her parents turn to look at each other before her little brother piped in.

"Can I go, too?" he asked. "I want to go with Amber."

"No!" they all said together.

"You're not old enough anyway," her dad told him. "They said volunteers had to be 16." He then turned back to Amber.

"Are you sure?" he asked.

"Yes, I want to go. I want to be a part of helping our country rebuild."

"Let us talk it over tonight," her mother said. "We'll let you know what we decide in the morning. I don't know if we want you going so far away when it's so hard to contact people now."

When Amber went to bed that night, it took her a long time to fall asleep. If her parents said no, she would almost feel relieved. Life would be the same as it was now, but with hope right around the corner. If they said yes, she would go have an adventure, even if the unknown scared her a bit. If Alex couldn't go, though, she wouldn't either. She didn't know if she could handle going on her own. She didn't feel that brave.

Amber's family all stayed home the next morning until the government men came around for their census. One of them had to verify where each person was sleeping in the house and another went to check the circuit breaker. Amber went with him into the basement to show him where it was. She held the flashlight to light up the wall while he wrote down some notes and then put a black metallic square sticker at the top of the box.

"What is that for?"

"The sticker? That's so if another team comes to do a census, they know another team was already here. We've been told to not just take anyone's word for it. Some people actually don't want their power turned back on."

"Really? Why wouldn't they want power?" she asked as they started to walk back upstairs.

"They've gotten used to how life is without it and don't

want it back on. For safety, though, we are required to put in the phone lines and the basic electrical power. They can decide if they want to use it later on. Even most of the Amish want the phone lines back on."

Amber heard her father giving the other man their birthdays and locations of birth as they emerged from the basement. She was going to have to have a shorter school day today so she could pack, and she still had to put together reading lists for her students, if her parents agreed to let her go.

"What should I pack if I want to volunteer to work with you guys?" she asked as the men turned to leave their house.

"Not much," the taller man said who had been talking to her father. "They have a lot of supplies there but you never can tell if you'll travel to the compound in West Virginia via airplane, truck or horse. You'll need a few changes of clothes, good walking shoes and a coat. We'd be glad to have you join the American Volunteer Corps – that's what it's officially called, but most people say AmVoc for short.

"We have to get on to the next house now." He turned to Amber. "See you tomorrow morning."

After the men left, Amber's father asked them all their plans for the day. It was their ritual since the power had gone off. Without cell phones, they only knew where people were by word-of-mouth or by searching. They decided early on that they would have a quick family meeting each morning to tell each other their plans. If anyone made a major diversion from his or her original plan, they were to try and get home and leave a note on the pad left on the kitchen table. It had come in handy more than once to know exactly where each family member was. They had started it after her dad had switched from being part of the hunting party one day to helping do patrols because Brian had the stomach flu and couldn't do it. When the hunting party came back without her dad, they all panicked until Mr. Rodriquez told them that he was out on patrol. Even though the entire neighborhood was in this together, her family would always look out for each other first and foremost.

"I'm helping with laundry in the morning and passing

out rations this afternoon," her mom said.

"I've got school," Amber's brother glared at her when he said it. "Then I'm on harvest duty."

"I'm on patrol today and then have to help with security at the rations," her father said. "If you see the workers at our house, they're going to install the phone line here since this is our indoor meeting space."

"I've got to run to the library, teach school and then … pack?" Amber said, still waiting on an answer from her parents.

Her parents looked at each other and then back to her. Her mom took her hand.

"I was hoping you'd have woken up and changed your mind, but your dad thought you might still want to go. We both really would rather have you stay, but you're 16 now and have had to grow up a lot this past year. We talked last night and decided to support you if you do want to go," Mom said.

"I really do. It would really help out with the food rations and I could be part of something historic – bringing America back," she said. "Dad, do you want me to tell the board that I'm going to work so they can fix the schedule or do you? I need to go see if Alex is going with me."

"I will – I have to check in with them before I go on patrol. We talked to Alex's parents last night and they are going to let him go, too. But, we're only letting you guys go because you'll be together," he said. He put his arm around Amber's shoulders. "It seems to all be happening so fast." "I'll see if we can get something for a dessert for tonight," Mom said, getting a little teary. "It does seem so sudden, but we'll enjoy a night together as a family tonight."

Amber gave her mom a hug and then they all started getting ready for the day. Amber felt a rush of excitement about getting to go.

Amber's first stop was next door to see Alex. She was really glad his parents were letting him go, too. She didn't know if she could be brave enough to leave her family completely on her own. They had talked to Shelley last night, too, but she didn't want to leave. She had been helping the Reeds and

Rodriguezes with their children after Susanna died. They were pretty sure no other adults would want to volunteer since almost everyone had a family to watch over. Nancy was alone, but she was a nurse and she had helped so many of them survive and was very much needed. Even Mrs. Sanders had people dependent on her since she was Mike's surrogate mother now. Plus, she was still holding out hope that her husband would be released from jail and come home.

She waited on the bottom stair of Alex's front porch and waited. She didn't want to knock on the door in case he was still talking to his parents. She only had to wait a minute before he came out.

"I can go," he said. "Can you?"

"Yes!" They hugged and then parted for their last day of work in the neighborhood.

Amber ran over to Mrs. Thompson's house, which Amber had nicknamed the library. She had brought one of the cherished blank pieces of paper from her room with her and a pencil. She only had nine students, but she really had seen them learn and grow over the past several months. When life was "normal" again, she'd be a teacher in a school where students had light and warmth from electricity – and where she could search the Internet for answers to all their questions. She knocked on the door and heard Mrs. Thompson tell her to come in.

"Hi, Mrs. Thompson. It's Amber. I just need to look at the books."

"Okay, dear. How are you?"

"I'm good. I've actually got to make a reading list for my students. I'm going to volunteer to work for the government and have to leave tomorrow."

"You're leaving us, dearie?"

"I am. Alex is going to come with me, too."

"I guess you have grown up over the past few years. I'll miss your visits."

"Thanks – I want to leave my students a reading list for while I'm gone. I'm guessing we'll be back soon after the power is all back on."

"I hope so. Your students will be welcome to any of the

books. Maybe I could do some school meetings with them here."

"That would be wonderful! We'll read chapter six of *Wind in the Willows* today. Maybe you could pick up where I leave off?"

"Sure. Can you write that down for me, though? I tend to forget. I always loved that book."

Amber finished her list of books, wrote down some notes about the students for Mrs. Thompson and said goodbye. She headed toward the "schoolhouse." She knew her students would be trickling in today after the military men did their census work. Only three students had beaten her to the Polk's house. She decided she'd tell the students as they showed up, give them their reading list and instructions, read the chapter of *Wind in the Willows* and then let them have the rest of the day off. She needed to get back and pack as soon as she could and she still had to help with harvesting for a bit. She got a few hoorays and a few tears when she told them that it was the last day of school for a while. She got big hugs from everyone, though, before she left. She put Samantha in charge of future "museum" tours and Austin was in charge of collecting book reports. She warned them that Mrs. Thompson might hold class at the "library" every so often, but she also told them that they were all very smart and with the power coming back on soon, the whole world would be back open to them.

When the last student left, Amber sat down in the schoolhouse and thought over her time teaching the children. She was surer than ever that she wanted to be a schoolteacher after she went to college. She wished she could have taken a picture of each student to take with her. She let a few tears fall, but then wiped them away and stood up to leave. She was going to miss home, but she knew she should go and help in another way for now.

After harvesting at the Speers' farm for two hours, she headed toward home to start packing. She found an old duffel bag with her name embroidered on it in the back of her closet. The last time she had used it was a week before the power went out when she spent the night at her friend Abby's house.

She hadn't thought about Abby for a while. She lived twenty-five minutes away – the other side of the school district – but that was now a world away. She wondered if she would run into anyone she knew at her government job.

She looked around her room and started laying stuff on her bed that she wanted to take – a picture of her family, a photo of Miss Gray, her journal, a teddy bear, a basic sewing kit, a few of her favorite books and several outfits. She knew she'd want her boots and coats, too, and her own pillow. She could stuff a few things in the pillowcase, too. She crammed it all in her duffel bag and pillowcase and then sat down on her bed. She had a few minutes at least to herself – a rarity in these times – and started to get nervous. Besides family vacations and the seventh grade overnight trip to the state capitol, she had never been away from home much. Now she was going away with only one person that she knew. She and Alex planned to stay together, but she had no guarantees as to what jobs they would each be assigned. She took a deep breath and did what she had done many times since the power went out – thought, "What is good about this?" She would make new friends. She would earn her family credits to make life better soon. The neighborhood would get more food. The power would come back on soon. She would be fed and warm.

"Amber, are you home?" she heard her brother call to her. She went to go see him, welcome for an interruption in her thoughts.

Amber's mom surprised them with a few brownies that night.

"Alex's mom and I found most of the ingredients in our pantries, but had to use applesauce from the Speers instead of oil and there was no vanilla. It doesn't have as much cocoa powder as normal either. They're really flat, too, since the baking powder is so old," her mom started rambling.

"Mom, this is wonderful! Thank you," Amber took a bite. Definitely not as chocolate tasting as "normal" brownies might be but they were delicious. "It's so good!"

It was a quiet dinner until Amber's brother suggested they play a game of Monopoly before going to bed. Several hours later, they were laughing at Dad's luck by landing on both Park Place and Boardwalk before going bankrupt. Amber knew she would miss her family. She had an oddly mixed feeling of excitement and nervousness. She tossed and turned most of the night. Her dad woke her up the next morning.

They went downstairs for a quick family breakfast and then it was time for Amber to leave. She asked them to say goodbye in the house.

"Be safe, Amber," her dad said. "Call often and come back soon."

"I will, Dad."

"I love you, Amber," her mom said, with a tissue in her hand.

"I love you all very much," Amber said as she took a good look at each one. It would be a while before she saw them again and she wanted to remember this moment.

After a few more hugs, she walked out the front door and wiped her tears away. Alex was waiting for her in the street.

"Are you ready?" he asked with a duffel bag slung over his shoulder.

"Guess I am," she said, hugging her pillowcase. "Let's go have an adventure."

CHAPTER TEN

The truck took Amber and Alex to a mall that was three hours away from where they lived. They had sat next to each other in the bed of the truck pointing out anything that caught their eye, but the truck was too loud to talk over. They saw one field that had several tents set up in the middle of it and they saw the remnants of an airplane crash. Amber had reached for Alex's hand when the saw the wreckage.

At the mall, Capt. Roberts passed them off to another military member, asking that man to arrange the rest of their travel to AmVoc. They were shown to some cots and told to put their belongings underneath.

"We could use some help with food distribution today. We had a lot of people show up yesterday. Are you two up for helping?"

Amber looked at Alex and nodded slightly.

"Sure," Alex replied for them. "We'd just like to stay together."

"We can do that."

The man took them to the sandwich making line, located in what looked like an old Sears store. A few very young looking military members were just starting to prep things for lunch. There were three folding tables set up in one long line and people were doing the same thing on both sides, except one side had peanut butter and the other had lunch meat for the sandwiches. Amber and Alex were put at the beginning of the line - putting two slices of bread on a paper plate. They finally got to talk to each other while doing the job. There were only 3 bags of bread left when they were told to stop.

"Now it's our turn," a young woman in uniform told Amber. "Get a plate and follow me down the line."

Alex came up behind Amber and they both picked up plates and bread. Amber put turkey on hers and Alex chose ham. Then, they each got an apple and some cooked carrots. Amber and Alex started heading toward the mall hallways where everyone else was eating.

"Hey, you two, come this way," the woman shouted at them. Alex lifted his eyebrow as he looked at Amber, but they both went back towards the woman.

"Since you helped, I get to show you where the good stuff is. You can only pick one, though."

She led them around a corner and pointed at some boxes lined up against a wall. Amber looked inside one and gasped. Alex peered over her shoulder.

"Oreos!" Alex said. There were small packages of all sorts of cookies and crackers.

"Shh," the woman said. "Not so loud. It's the secret stash for volunteers. We don't have enough to go around for everyone."

Alex took a package of Oreos and Amber reached for the chocolate chip cookies. Then they followed the woman to a set of tables set up out of view of anyone who could peak into the Sears store.

Amber and Alex sat off by themselves and savored every bite of a lunch unlike anything they'd had since the power went out. They even split their cookies; giving the other person three so they could both have some of each kind. Alex closed his eyes as he took the first bite of the Oreo.

"Heaven," he sighed. Amber laughed, almost spitting out her cookie.

They spent the afternoon helping the military members take inventory and then helped hand out MREs for dinner. When it was their turn to pick, Amber chose spaghetti and Alex chose chilimac. They were allowed to pick another cookie package, too.

"I can't believe out of all the choices, you still picked chilimac," Amber said as they were setting up the heaters for their food. "I think I only had spaghetti once but I'd be glad to never eat the chilimac again."

"Really? I love the stuff," Alex said. "My mom used to make it all the time growing up. It's not as good as hers, of course, but it reminds me of it."

"Was that your favorite dish your mom made?"

"Hmm, probably only second to bacon cheeseburgers."

"I loved when my mom made chicken fried rice."

"I bet they'll be ready to make those meals for us when we get back home."

"I hope so."

They spent that night at the mall and were woken up early to get on another truck that drove them to a military base in Virginia. They were taken to a cafeteria and fed lunch before being put in a van that had no windows in the back. They sat next to each other and played some word games to pass the time. Every time they tried to ask someone when they would arrive, they were ignored. They were given peanut butter sandwiches and an apple each when it was time for dinner. They were starting to fall asleep, leaning on each other, when the van stopped. The doors opened and they were told to get out. They were at a gate and several armed military men checked each of them over, looked in their bags and searched the entire van.

Amber wondered where exactly they were. She didn't see anything but trees on both sides of the fence. She saw Alex looking around, too. He looked at her and shrugged. They were told to get back in the van and they both craned their necks to try and look out the front windows as they drove on. It was almost ten minutes before they saw a compound of three large concrete buildings lit up by the streetlamps. Each building was five stories tall. They drove completely around to the back of the buildings and went down into a tunnel. The drive in the tunnel took several minutes before they stopped in what looked like a parking garage – complete with electric lights instead of candles.

"Welcome to AmVoc," the soldier told them as he

helped them out of the truck. They got their bags from the back of the truck and waited to be told what to do next. The soldier was busy talking to two mechanics at the nearby office.

"All I want is a shower and a bed," Amber said to Alex. He just nodded and yawned.

"Hey, kids," the soldier called to them. "Follow me and I'll show you where you'll start out."

They followed him up two flights of stairs and down a hallway. He knocked on a door that had a piece of paper taped on it with "Quarantine Check In" written on it. A woman in khaki pants and a white polo opened the door.

"Why do you military guys always bring the new ones in so late?" she sighed and opened the door wide for Amber and Alex to enter. Amber wondered exactly how late it was.

"Just doing what I'm told, Ma'am," he replied and then left.

"Don't sit down," the woman told them as they moved toward the chairs. "I just need to get some basic information and then I'll take you to your rooms."

She gave them each a form on a clipboard that asked for their name, age, hometown, medical conditions and skills. Within minutes, they handed the forms back and she glanced them over quickly.

"Amber, you stay here while I take Alex to the men's section," she said.

"When will I see Amber again?" Alex asked her.

"That all depends on what job you're assigned. It could be a while."

"Our parents only let us come because we're supposed to be working together," Amber said, worried about being separated from Alex.

They lady sighed.

"They are supposed to tell you there are no guarantees of work placement. For right now, we always separate the girls and boys for quarantine time. It usually only lasts a few days. Then when you are given your aptitude tests, we will assign you a job."

Amber and Alex looked at each other. Amber's stomach

started hurting and she started twisting her hands together. She saw Alex had a smile on his face, though.

"I'll be okay, Amber," he said as he put his hand on her arm. "We're both at the same location and I'll find a way to get in touch with you. I promise."

She gave him big hug and as they let go, Alex kissed her forehead. She watched as the woman led Alex down a hallway. Amber hoped she would see him again soon, but she had a feeling it was going to be a while. It was all out of her control now, though. Amber tried to distract herself while they were gone by looking around the woman's office. There wasn't anything personal except for a Mickey Mouse pen sitting on top of a stack of brown folders. The black laptop was closed and the clipboards she and Alex had used were on the middle of the desk. Amber wondered if the woman had a family and where she was from.

When the woman returned, Amber was taken to an exam room that looked like a small hospital room. A woman with a blond ponytail in green scrubs told her to take a shower and dress in a pair of matching scrubs. She was then was given a complete physical with blood work to make sure she didn't have any "bugs or communicable diseases" by a different nurse who didn't look happy to be assigned to her current duties. Amber decided it would be better not to ask her any questions. She was then shown to her room. She could barely keep her eyes open by then and went to sleep with just a quick glance around the room.

Amber was allowed to keep her journal, but all her other belongings had to be quarantined as well. She actually really enjoyed her first full day in quarantine. It was the first time since the power went out that she could just rest and not worry about anything. Three times a day, the nurse stopped in with food and asked her how she was doing and if she wanted anything in particular. She had her own bathroom and shower, complete with all the toiletries she needed. While the walls were plain, there was a desk and chair where there were books, old magazines, a pad of paper and pencils. There were several pairs of scrubs and undergarments just her size that she could change into every day. The lights would dim and get brighter according to the time of day she was told by the nurse the first morning. When it got dark, she slept and then the light would wake her up in the morning. There was no clock in the room. She tried to keep herself from thinking about her family and all they were going through back home. She couldn't help but think of her brother when they brought her some ice cream on the third day. It was even his favorite flavor – chocolate chip cookie dough. She made note of it in her journal that night and gave in to a few tears from missing her family and friends. She wondered if Alex was feeling the same.

Shortly after the lights got brighter on the fourth day, there was a knock at her door and the same blond nurse who she saw the first day slowly opened the door.

"Please shower and get dressed in these clothes as quickly as possible. You have passed your physical and just need a few supplements and vitamins to get you in tip-top shape. We'll get you assigned to a work duty and room today after testing."

The nurse dumped some clothes right inside the door, put a breakfast tray on her desk and then left. Amber was relieved she would be moving on to the working part of being there. She was starting to get bored with having nothing to do but relax. She also felt herself hoping she would see Alex today. When Amber went to get dressed, she saw there was a pair of white Keds, white socks, white underwear and sports bra, khaki pants and a light blue polo shirt with AVC embroidered in red on the front left. Amber showered and changed and then waited for the woman to come back. Something her father used to say came to her head – hurry up and wait. He was always annoyed when he said that and she now understood the feeling. She started to wonder how her family was doing without her, but quickly changed her train of thought to what kind of work duty she could be put on. Every time she thought of her family during her quarantine, she felt guilty. Her life was so easy right now compared to how it had been those months without power.

The woman came back and told Amber to follow her. She was first taken to a room to have an ID badge made. It was attached to a red lanyard with AVC in white repeated over and over along it.

"Keep this with you at all times. It lets us know where you are, opens your room door, keeps track of your rations and lets people know you are supposed to be here."

Then she was dropped off at the testing room. While the badge room had been empty when she entered and only two other people came in after her, the testing room was full.

"This is Amber Birch. I think she's the last in Batch Sierra72," the woman told an older man sitting behind a desk just inside the testing room. He opened a notebook and checked something off. Then he looked up at his computer screen and used his mouse to click a few things.

"What is your ID number?" he asked Amber. The woman who had brought her to the room walked off without saying goodbye.

"AF3274," Amber read off her badge.

"Thanks," he replied after he typed it into the computer and wrote it in the notebook. He then looked at her and smiled.

"Welcome to the American Volunteer Corps Center. This is the Testing Room. We will use the results to determine where your skills will best be used. There are twelve stations. You will start at the Station 1 line and work your way around. There will be a break at meal times. Remember to swipe your card at each station. When you are done, you will wait in the room through Door A for your work duty and room assignments. There will be no talking except when asked questions at the stations. Any questions?"

Amber shook her head no and then he told her to go ahead to Station 1.

Amber got in line behind six other people – two girls about her age, one man around her father's age, two older men and one older woman. A boy her age was being asked questions behind a screen, which she peeked around under the guise of tying her shoe. She could see an eye chart and guessed she would have her vision checked. She had always had good eyesight. Her mother always jokingly told her she had "true blue eagle eyes."

She started looking around the room for Alex. Surely he had been in quarantine about the same time as her. She scanned the room quickly twice and then did a slow look, making sure she saw each person who left a station. No Alex. In fact, she noticed only half of the people in the room were around her age and only about three of those were boys. Those boys were very scrawny and wore glasses. She guessed Alex had been assigned a work duty right away that didn't need a complete physical screening – manual labor. She groaned inwardly. On their journey, he had said many times that manual labor was the one thing he wouldn't want to do at AmVoc unless he could work with cars. He had been studying any engineering book he could during his spare time since the power went off and wanted to be on the front lines of rebuilding the country and running power in a better way. She'd have to figure out a way to find out where he was. They hadn't talked about being separated at all.

Amber spent a lot of time reassuring herself that Alex was okay while she waited in line after line. She spent some time rereading her journal, too, which helped remind her why she was at AmVoc – to help make things better back home.

The stations covered her eyesight, hearing, reading comprehension, writing abilities, balance, foreign language experience, weight lifting, typing skills, personality, CPR knowledge, hand-eye coordination and she had to choose from a long list of life experiences to see what she had or hadn't done. Some of the stations were actually a little on the fun side, like walking down a balance beam and doing the personality tests. She still had two stations left when dinner was brought in. It was hard to know what time it was because there were no clocks and the lights stayed bright all the time in the testing room. They all sat down in the chairs in the next room and were handed a tray. Amber enjoyed the grilled chicken sandwich with a side salad and orange slices. They were offered milk or water and Amber chose the cold milk. Amber savored every bite and noticed everyone else was eating slowly, too. After the trays were collected, a man in a suit came in and announced that those who had not finished their assessments within two more hours would go back to quarantine for the night and then come back in the morning. Those who finished would get their job and room assignments. Amber hoped she would finish and actually managed to with just fifteen minutes to spare, the last station tester told her. The two others who came into the badge room after her were the only others left when she was finished. After the last station, she went to sit in the next room and wait "quietly" for her assignments.

Amber heard her name called just a few minutes after she sat down in the next room. She had actually started to doze off. She had been wondering if she would have a room to herself. Maybe she would have roommates or maybe it would be a big room with lots of beds. When she stood up and looked at the woman, she was surprised to see her fifth grade teacher, Mrs. Robertson.

"Mrs. Robertson?" Amber said, smiling and started to move to give her a hug but Mrs. Robertson had already started walking back out the door. She looked the same to Amber except for the clothing. She had always worn long skirts to school. It was a little odd to see her in pants. Her brown hair was still up in a bun, though.

"Please follow me quickly, Amber," Mrs. Robertson said coldly.

Amber wondered why she wasn't being friendlier, but maybe she didn't recognize her anymore. She followed Mrs. Robertson down the hall.

"Please listen carefully as I don't have much time to explain before lights out time. I do remember you, Amber, but we'll have to catch up another time. I'm sorry – it's been a very long day again and I'm very tired. Quotas mean credits. You have scored in the high range from your evaluation, so you will be on Phone Duty. You will answer phone calls and help citizens find answers to their questions. You will have two days to study the answer books, one day of training and then you'll start your shift. You will work four days and have one day off. On your day off, you may visit the store, lounge room, computer room and library, and you can make one phone call home if it's your turn. You will work a twelve-hour shift each day and your roommate will work the opposite shift so you won't be in the room when the other needs to sleep. There is more to your new life, but I have only five minutes to report back to my boss. Remember to ask someone to give you the introduction briefing tomorrow. You didn't have time for it today."

They stopped just then in front of door Z273H and Amber saw her bag and pillowcase beside the door.

"You use your keycard to open it," Mrs. Robertson said. Amber did just that and saw a small, but neat and tidy room. "I would recommend getting in and settled right away. The lights will turn off automatically very soon. They dim before-hand and will get brighter when it is time to wake up, just like in quarantine. They have UV light in them to help you adjust to life underground. Someone will be by to get you in the morning to show you where to study. I hope we run into each other soon."

Mrs. Robertson put her hand on Amber's shoulder and smiled at her. Amber almost sensed some pity in the smile and look, but then Mrs. Robertson started walking away.

Amber felt dazed with all the information Mrs. Robertson had given her. She picked up her bag and pillowcase and brought them into the room. There were two cot-sized beds with a small nightstand between them. There was a lamp over each bed. At the other end of the room were two lockers. She could tell the bed by the door was hers – the other had a small purple turtle stuffed animal and pink pillow on it. One of the lockers was open and empty, so she assumed that one was hers, too. Across from the door was another door with the word "Toilet" on it. She quickly peeked in and saw a small sink, toilet and standing-room-only shower. She noticed the lights behind her in the room start dimming. She quickly rummaged through her bag for pajamas and her toothbrush. She changed and brushed her teeth, emptied her pillowcase into her locker, found her teddy bear and climbed onto her cot just as it got dark. There were small strips of light by the doors, but other than that, it was dark and quiet. She started to wish she had time to journal about the day, but was asleep before she could even finish the thought.

CHAPTER ELEVEN

Amber was startled awake by the sound of banging on her door.

"Amber, open up," a voice shouted. She immediately sat up in bed not knowing where she was. The lights were on, but slightly dim, and the room was unfamiliar. Was she dreaming?

The pounding on the door started again. It wasn't a dream.

"Coming. Just a sec," she shouted back. She opened the door to find a short woman standing there.

"You are to report for training manual study in ten minutes. Room 25C. Breakfast will be over shortly. Please change into clothes rather quickly if you want to eat," the woman said. She was dressed in khaki pants, a dark blue polo shirt, simple brown shoes and her hair in a bun. Her lanyard was white with AVC in red lettering. She shut the door on Amber, who still felt slightly confused about the whole situation. She threw her pajamas on her bed, put on some jeans and a shirt, brushed her teeth and opened up her door. The woman was waiting across the hallway with her back against the wall and arms crossed against her chest. She looked Amber up and down, which made Amber feel self-conscious.

"That'll do for now," she said. "You'll get more uniforms later today. Follow me."

She started walking and then turned back to look at Amber.

"Hey, do you have your identification card?" the woman scowled. Amber knew she expected her to say she had forgotten it.

Amber felt her neck and felt relief when she felt the lanyard. She must have slept with it on. She pulled the card out from under her shirt.

"Yep," she said. "Right here."

Amber followed her down several hallways when the lady stopped in front of swinging brown doors with the word "cafeteria" across both doors.

"Breakfast is right in there," the lady said. She looked down at her watch. "You have five minutes. Just use your keycard – be quick! Then go to the room down there – 25C." The woman pointed down the hall to the right and then walked away.

Amber walked through the doors and was instantly overwhelmed. The amount of food she saw reminded her of buffet restaurants her parents used to take them to when they would celebrate good report card grades. Her stomach rumbled but she couldn't make herself move. A voice snapped her out of her daze.

"I'm sorry – what did you say?" she turned to her right where the voice was coming from. There stood a boy about her age with dark hair and blue eyes. "First time?" he asked.

"Yes, and I'm supposed to be done in five minutes – might be three now. Then Room 25C."

"Here, come with me." He took her to the second aisle, put a cereal bar and banana on a plate and walked up to a lady standing in front of a computer.

"You just have to show her your identification card," he said.

She showed it and the lady scanned it without saying a word. The boy then walked over to a long table, just like they had at her high school lunchroom.

"Eat quickly and I'll show you where to go," he said. "I'll go get you a bottle of water."

"Thanks!" she said and started eating. She had not had a banana for more than a year and the cereal bar was delicious with raspberry filling in it. She wanted to savor each bite, but forced herself to hurry. He brought her back a water bottle just as she was finishing the cereal bar.

"Here you go. Drink this while we walk to the training room," he said. As he pushed open the door, he turned back to her and asked if she had been given a pair of earplugs.

"Earplugs?"

"Yeah, like the kind they use around airplanes. Make sure to ask someone for them before you go to bed or you won't be sleeping soon."

"What? Why is that?"

"Listen."

They stood still in the middle of the doorway and she heard non-stop noise. There was people talking, the hum of electricity, footsteps, doors opening and closing.

"We all got used to the silence before we came here. You'll need to block out the noise to sleep."

She nodded since what he said made sense. She hadn't had any trouble sleeping yet as she'd been so tired from the traveling. They started walking down the hall. They only had to pass three doorways until they were at 25C.

"You go here. By the way, if I see you again, I'm Drew," he reached out to shake her hand.

"Thanks, Drew. I'm Amber," she said, shook his hand and then turned to walk into Room 25C.

The door creaked when she opened it and everyone in the room turned back to look at her. She knew immediately that she was late. The room was bare except for a whiteboard at the front and a few rows of folding chairs in the middle.

"So glad you could join us," said the man in front. He had short black hair that was spiked up a little and wore wire glasses. "Your name?"

"I'm Amber Birch. Sorry to be late. I just got a room last ..."

"Please sit down," he said, interrupting her sternly. "I'm Mr. Quinn and I'm in charge of the Phone Section of AmVoc. You'll have to have someone catch you up later. Get a notebook and pencil from the back table and find a seat. Now, where was I?"

Amber picked up a notebook and pencil and wondered if anyone was happy in this place. Actually, Drew had seemed fairly happy. He seemed a bit tired, but at least he didn't seem rushed. She looked at the chairs and realized she had to sit in the front row. There were about twenty people sitting in folding chairs and only two others were in the front row. No one even made eye contact with her as she made her way to a chair. It looked like everyone had already taken a bunch of notes, but she couldn't have been more than a few minutes late. She noticed she was the only one not wearing the khaki and polo uniform.

"We have a study room for you trainees to use for the next two days. Manuals have been created to help you find answers to the questions you will be asked. You need to become familiar with how the manuals are organized. They will be at your workstation once you begin in three days. It's a quick process, but we have several workers about to finish their commitment and they want to return to their families. The study room is built to model the workstations. We will give you a ten-minute rest break every two hours and breaks for meals. Your twelve-hour shifts begin today, though. Please take this seriously. You will have people calling who are desperate for answers. Follow me and let's begin."

Mr. Quinn walked to a door on the left side of the room and opened a door marked Training. They followed him through the door and saw a room filled with partitioned desks. Each desk had two phones and a dozen thick binders on a shelf above the phone. There were several pencils, a bottle of water and a mug for coffee at each desk. There was also a nametag with two names on it attached to the shelf.

"Find your nametag, sit and start studying. I'll be back at break. No talking. Remember what you can earn by working well."

Amber wondered what exactly he meant by that. She remembered Captain Roberts saying something about earning credits for your family, but no one had explained to her how that would all work. She made a mental note to ask Mr. Quinn at the first break. She found her desk and sat down.

The binders were arranged by topic: Phone system, First

Aid, Gardening, Food Safety, Small Appliance Repair, Atlases, Pest Control, Edible Plants, Water, Law, Government, Miscellaneous. She picked up the Miscellaneous binder first and quickly realized the binder was an afterthought. The topics in the binder were arranged in no particular order and were often copies of handwritten notes. The first page was labeled "How to Properly Cook Squirrel," which made Amber feel queasy. The next was "Reloading Ammo" and the one after that was "Warnings against Home Distillation."

The other books were more organized and gave sample questions in relation to the topic presented, except the Atlases binder, which was a collection of maps for the entire Eastern United States. She decided she would need to ask for a magnifying glass to read some of the maps and then found one in the pocket at the back of the binder. There were red stars marking military bases and blue stars marking shopping malls. She guessed she might get some calls asking for directions.

She had flipped through the Phone System binder and was starting on the First Aid one when Mr. Quinn came back in and told them they had a ten-minute break. Water, coffee and an assortment of fruit and granola bars were on a table in the back of the room. Amber noticed Mr. Quinn walking back toward the door and she ran up to catch him before he left.

"Mr. Quinn, I have a few questions."

"Oh, yes, you probably do. You're the late one. You could just ask one of these other trainees to share their notes with you."

"Yes, sir, I will do that, but I was told to tell someone that I still need the introduction briefing. I got to my room right before lights out last night and didn't get to attend one."

Mr. Quinn sighed and looked at his watch.

"You'll have to go to one on your day off. There's no time during training to attend that briefing. They drag it out for two hours usually. Go to room 37G on your day off at 3 p.m. and they'll have the newcomer briefing then."

She said thank you as he started to leave and wrote down what he said in her notebook. Then she walked over to the snack table and picked up an apple.

"Where are you from?" Amber jumped a little. She hadn't seen the girl walk up. The girl had long, straight black hair. Amber instinctively reached up to her own brown curls. She had cut hers to her shoulders a few weeks after the power went out, along with almost all the women in the neighborhood. Between the lack of hot running water and the heat, long hair had been an annoyance and they kept it short.

"I'm from North Carolina. You?"

"I'm from Northeast Pennsylvania. I'm Natasha."

"I'm Amber. Would you mind sharing your notes with me from what I missed this morning?"

"Sure. Let's do that on the next break. Looks like our time is almost up."

After the first break, they were given another two binders. One was full of questions that had already been called in and they were supposed to try and find the answers in the binders. The other was full of blank forms – the ones they would fill out during the phone calls. The front page had spaces for the callers' questions and then what responses were given. The back of the form had questions about their location, number of people alive near them, number of people who had died and when and what kind of food drops they had received.

Amber started reading through the questions that had already been called in. Some were easy, straightforward questions about sanitation or first aid. Others seemed desperate and asked about eating tree bark and coyote bites on a toddler. She was almost at the end of the question binder when she felt a tap on her shoulder.

"Ms. Birch," Mr. Quinn said. "Did you want to take your lunch break or keep on reading?"

Amber glanced quickly around her and realized everyone else was gone.

"Oh, I didn't hear that it was time for lunch," she said as she stood up. She noticed he was smiling at her. "How much time do I have left?"

"You still have forty-five minutes. Do you remember how to get to the cafeteria?"

"Yes, sir," Amber said. "Thank you."

"Also, I assume you didn't get uniforms since you didn't get the newcomer briefing. I made a call and they will deliver them to your room by tonight." Then he walked back toward his desk.

She was surprised at the change in Mr. Quinn's demeanor. He didn't seem as gruff as he first had in the morning. Maybe he wasn't a morning person, she thought. It reminded her of her brother. She had told her mom she wouldn't wake him up anymore in the morning after he almost hit her once. He was never quite himself until he'd been awake for at least an hour.

Amber was amazed by how many choices she had for lunch. She picked out some pizza, a salad with ranch dressing and a piece of apple pie. After scanning her card, she quickly scanned the cafeteria for an open spot before finding a seat in a corner. She looked for Natasha and Drew, but didn't see them anywhere. Once she sat down, she realized she wasn't going to mind being by herself – she was going to enjoy this meal. She wanted to savor every bite. It had been so long since she'd eaten pizza.

Natasha found her shortly after she finished eating. She had a tray with a salad, grilled cheese and water.

"Hey! Amber, right?"

"Yes. And you're Natasha."

"Can I sit with you? We could go over what you missed while I eat."

"Sure. I looked around for you when I sat down, but I didn't see you."

"I ran to the store real quick to get a new book. I read all of mine waiting for training to start. I finished quarantine three days ago."

"The store has books? Jeez, I think I'm going to need a tour, too. I haven't even done the introductory briefing yet. Mr. Quinn said I'll have to do that on my next day off."

"Yep, you do have a lot to catch up on. I'll help you, though."

In between bites, Natasha told her how their shift would work. They were on the day shift and work was from 8 a.m.

to 8 p.m. with a morning and afternoon fifteen-minute break and a forty-five-minute lunch and dinner break. Only a quarter of them would break at a time so the phones would still be mostly manned. Lights were off at 10 p.m. and turned on at 7 a.m. They would work for four days with one day off. Other workers at AmVoc had special duty to cover the phones on their day off. Anything not covered in the manual could be brought to their supervisor's attention. She gave her a quick review of how the phones worked, too. There were hold and transfer buttons and they could have three lines waiting on each phone, labeled 1, 2 and 3.

"Oh, and when you answer the phone, you have to say, 'AmVoc Citizen Help Line. This is Natasha. How can I help you?'" Natasha said it in a very professional sounding voice that had them both giggling.

They walked back to the training room together and got there just in time. Amber was glad to not be late for once.

The first two training days passed quickly and even though Amber was tired at night from the long shift, she was restless from sitting all day long. They had more binders to work through and then they did practice calls with each other and a test with Mr. Quinn or another supervisor, Mr. Fray. She had discovered some earplugs on top of her uniforms when she got back the first night. She slept much better with them in. She must have been so tired the first few days there that her body wasn't bothered by the noise. She thought of Drew when she put them in and hoped she would see him sometime soon. She was really missing Alex and wondered if there was a way she could get in touch with him. She'd have to remember to ask Natasha how to do it when they had time to talk.

Her first workdays went by in a blur, and while she ate lunch and dinner with Natasha on the remaining two training days, they were so rushed and tired that she forgot about asking her if there was a way to get in touch with Alex. They planned to meet for breakfast on the first day off and Amber was going to ask her then. They had to start working their four-day shift right after the three days of training. By the morning of her first day off, Amber was exhausted. She left her room just a little after 8 a.m. that morning.

"Hey, you must be Amber, right?"

Amber had opened her room door to see a teenager with short, red hair staring at her. She had two other girls standing beside her who were all glaring at Amber.

"Yeah, I'm Amber. Who are you?"

"I'm your roommate, Marissa. And I would appreciate it if you could keep your part of the room clean, okay? I'm tired of coming to my room and having it look like someone else's – I've been here almost a year now and that room has been mine the whole time. You just sleep there, okay?"

Before Amber could even say a word, the three girls turned around and walked away. Amber closed the room door behind her and just stared at the girls and shook her head. She really didn't leave a mess in the room at all. She made her bed and kept her things in her locker. She kept her uniform on her chair and a book on her nightstand, but that was it.

"Don't worry about them," a girl said as she walked toward Amber and looked at her with pity in her eyes. She had walked out of her room a few doors down right after Amber had left hers. "Marissa doesn't get along with anyone except her two buddies, Mandy and Lysa. They've all been here from the beginning, so they act like they own the place. Lysa is my roommate and tries to take over our room like it's all hers. I just put her stuff on her bed when I get in the room and keep my important things tucked away."

"Thanks. I'm not used to someone acting so rude. She's not the first person I've met around here that's been like that. I saw an old teacher of mine when I first came here and she acted so strange."

"Most people around here are just really tired," she said. "I'm Jessie."

"I'm Amber. I know I'm tired and I've only been working here a few days. I just finished my first work week."

"That's rough. It helps, though, to see what all we're accomplishing at the update briefing. They let us know the current death toll, how the airdrops are going, the infrastructure rebuild status and the citizenship recall numbers."

"Update briefing? Citizenship recall?"

"You haven't heard about that? Where did you come from?"

"North Carolina – but about two hours from any of the big cities."

"Oh, I came from near Baltimore. We were kept up to date on the news with a weekly airdrop."

"Weekly? We only had one every few months. Every week would have been nice. How long have you been working here?"

"I got here about four months ago. I'm just working for the college deal."

"The college deal?"

"Oh, wow – you don't even know about the college deal? Why did you come work here then? Never mind that – I have a lot to catch you up on. Let's go get something to eat while we talk."

Natasha joined Amber and Jessie for breakfast. Jessie gave them an overview of what they would hear at the update briefings.

It turned out that Amber had missed a lot by not getting the newcomer briefing right away. Each day off, she was supposed to report to an auditorium at 9 a.m. to hear the latest updates on the country. The people in charge had found out quickly that the workers at AmVoc wanted to know how the outside world was doing to know if they were making a difference. They showed where the airdrops had taken place over the past week, where the power had been restored, the death toll numbers and how many citizens had been brought back to the country from overseas locations.

"You're saying more than 25 million people have died since the power outage?" Amber said, finding it hard to grasp. That was ten times as many as was reported in the newspapers the workers had brought to her neighborhood.

"Yes, it's one of the saddest things about what happened," Jessie replied.

"Why don't they send that news out to everyone?" Amber asked.

"They don't want people to lose hope. But without power it's so hard to keep things sanitized so a lot of people have died from bad food or infections," Jessie told them. "The first huge loss was people in hospitals. We had a teenager in our neighborhood die because they couldn't find any insulin for him after they ran out."

"Oh no. I'm sorry to hear that, Jessie. We had an elderly woman and baby die during the winter. There was also a girl my age that died from an infection from a cut. It's just so hard to fathom that many people gone," Amber said. Amber felt herself tear up, but tried to control her emotions so the others wouldn't see. She forced herself to focus on something else.

"The citizenship recall has been hard, though," Jessie said. "The government wants all Americans back in the country to help in some way or they will have their citizenships revoked."

"Wouldn't they want to come back and help?" Natasha asked.

"Would you want to leave a land of Internet, power and refrigerators to come here?" Jessie replied. "I have a cousin who was studying abroad in Denmark when it happened. She decided to become a citizen of that country instead of being forced to come back."

"Oh, I see." Amber's mind filled with so many questions, but she didn't want to bother Jessie too much after just meeting her. There was one thing Jessie had said that had really caught Amber's attention, though. "Can you tell me more about the college deal?"

"Sure. So, by working here, you can earn credits for ten families of your choice to get new appliances. That's if you only work for one year. If you work for two years, you can go to college for free, too. Then, if you can finish three years here, you can also earn a new car," Jessie explained.

"Free college?" Amber was amazed. "I've been dreaming of college since the fourth grade. I had only heard about the appliance credits. I can get through two years here for college."

"That's what I'm doing, too," Jessie said. "I've been

here for almost a year now, but I'm going to stay for the second year. I don't know if I need a car badly enough to stick around for a third year. By that point, they might not even need us anymore."

"So, what else do I need to know?" Amber said.

"They did bring you in to work fast. Most of us who have been here longer had a sponsor assigned to us that showed us the ropes. They just focus on putting you new people to work right away now. Did you know you could take classes on your day off? Plus, there is a crafting/sewing room. And, did anyone show you where to go on the computer to request books or magazines?"

"What?" Amber almost shouted at them, making both Natasha and Jessie jump in their seats. "I love to sew and read! What kinds of classes are there?"

"Let's just go give her a tour," Jessie said to Natasha.

The two of them started laughing and Amber joined in. They showed her where she could sew (her uniforms would soon be showing her personality a bit more), how to order the books she wanted and where the bulletin board with the class list was. She could also sign up to teach a class and asked them if any of them would want to learn to sew from her. Jessie said she would, but Natasha doubted she would be any good at it.

On the bulletin board, there were items for sale and people wanting to trade books. There were flyers for a book club, writing club, chess club and history club. People also offered lessons for school topics or sewing. The sewing lessons caught her eye, though. There were two posters for that, but neither was offered on her day-off cycle. She quickly made a sign-up sheet to see if anyone on her day-off cycle would be interested in lessons. That would be a fun way to pass the time. She also jotted down some book titles she'd be willing to swap on those flyers.

They finished up the tour just in time to get to the update briefing. The numbers matched what Jessie had told them that morning about how many people had died. But, there was a huge focus on how much had been accomplished – food drops and power restored to thousands of homes.

The three spent the rest of the day together, with Natasha and Jessie mainly asking Amber if she knew about this or knew about that. By the end of the day, she finally felt like she knew her way around AmVoc, or at least the areas she was allowed to go. It was a bigger area than she thought. Any hallway marked with red tape on the ground was okay for the phone division workers to go. Her lanyard being red made more sense to her now. She just had to make sure never to set foot in a hallway with black tape – that was where classified activity went on and she would be sent home immediately if she crossed into those areas. Jessie introduced them to some other teens working the phone lines. They were all on the same work cycle, so they would see each other on days off, except for Jessie. She worked in the cafeteria and their schedule would only match up once or twice a month. Since they were on their feet all day, they worked three days on and one day off.

By the time Amber needed to get to the newcomer briefing, her friends had told her most of what she heard there. She had to fill out paperwork with her intentions of working one, two or three years. She chose two and signed knowing her parents would agree that free college was worth the time. She had heard them talking many nights and knew they were worried about how the bills and mortgage would work once the power came back on. They were sure that somehow they would have to make back payments.

Amber went to her room that night feeling much more hopeful about life at AmVoc. At least she knew that she wouldn't run into her roommate very often since they worked opposite shifts and she now knew several other teenagers. Hopefully two years would go by quickly. She hoped she'd be able to call home soon. She would be able to receive messages from home, but they needed to know her ID number. She would need to check the message center the night before her day off to see if her turn was the next day. During the introduction briefing, they also mentioned she could send letters home, but there was no guarantee on any delivery as mail was only delivered if there was extra room on trucks and planes going to destinations. She wondered how they were all doing and planned to write a letter to them in the next few days.

She started reading a new book Jessie had let her borrow, *Christy* by Catherine Marshall, just as the lights started to dim. She sighed and then sat up in bed, realizing she forgot to ask how she could contact Alex. She would have to ask Natasha first thing in the morning. She felt really bad that she kept forgetting. She thought that maybe her brain was just taking on too much new information, but it didn't make her feel any better.

CHAPTER TWELVE

Amber was determined to ask about how to contact Alex the next day. She didn't see Natasha at breakfast, but at lunch they ended up on the same break and Amber asked Natasha as soon as they sat down to eat. She was worried about where they had placed him. Her hunch was that they had him working on mechanical things. He hadn't wanted to but he was knowledgeable about it.

"I'm sure there's a lot of people working to keep this place running, plus, I've overheard someone in the cafeteria talking about the auto repair center. He had been transferred from there and was talking about missing the sunlight," Natasha said.

Natasha had two ideas to track Alex down. One was to ask at the message center if they could look up his name.

"Or, you could ask Mr. Quinn to help you," she suggested.

"It might be easier with Mr. Quinn – if he's in a good mood," Amber said. "I wonder if they're even allowed to give out people's info at the message center."

"Well, let's check there before lunch is over and then we'll know," Natasha said. They quickly finished their meal and headed to the message center. There was only one other person in line, which was good as they had about seven minutes to report back to work.

"May I help you?" the woman behind the counter asked. She had short, gray curly hair and thick glasses.

"I'm wondering if I can find a way to see where a friend of mine ended up working," Amber said. "His name is …"

"I'm sorry, dear, but we can't give out personal information. You can leave a note with his name but I can only deliver it if he's at this AmVoc location and I can't tell you if he is or not."

Amber sighed. "Okay, well, thank you."

"You should still leave a note," Natasha said as they walked back to the Phone Center.

"I probably will later, but I'll see about asking Mr. Quinn first. I'd like to know for sure that a note would get to him."

At dinner, Amber ate alone as Natasha was still working. She came up with a plan to butter up Mr. Quinn the next day to ask him about Alex. A few candy bars bought at the cafeteria and left at his desk would help his mood. She'd already seen that happen once. When Mr. Quinn was in a bad mood, he would nitpick everything they did all day long, which was honestly most days so far. However, she saw two other girls sneak a candy bar on his desk during a break a few days ago and his mood completely changed for the rest of the day.

Each week, they would get $50 credited to their account for food and other items they wanted at the store located next to the cafeteria that Jessie and Natasha had shown her on her tour. There was often money left over at the end of the week, though, and that is what people used to pay for lessons, phone line numbers or to buy books from the newcomers at AmVoc. There was a transfer station set up on a laptop in the lounge area where students could use their keycards to transfer money to another person's account. Amber didn't spend much and planned to try and save up as much as she could as they could withdraw their balance when they left AmVoc. Finding Alex was worth buying a few candy bars, though.

"What's his name?" Mr. Quinn asked after Amber told him her story the next morning at the first break. She had watched as he entered the room shortly after their shift started and saw him smile at the four candy bars on his desk in the front corner of the room.

"Alex McCarthy," Amber replied.

"Okay, I'll see what I can find. Come see me at the end of your shift."

Amber didn't want to wait that long, but she wasn't going to push Mr. Quinn. Breaks and lunches had "accidentally" been cut short when he was in a bad mood.

She was fairly hopeful she would be in contact with Alex soon, though. Her hopeful mood lasted most of the morning until she picked up the phone and heard crying at the end.

"Hello. This is Amber at AmVoc. How can I..."

"Help us! Please! Help us!" a woman's voice cried.

"What do you need help with?"

"There's no more food. We're so hungry. My children will barely move. We need food."

"I'm so sorry to hear that. When is the last time you had an airdrop?"

"We've never had an airdrop."

"Never?"

"No – we haven't gotten any food. The letter said there would be food. There's no food! Does anyone care whether we live?"

"Did they leave food when they put in your phone line?"

"No. Didn't I just tell you? There hasn't been any food!"

"Ma'am, I've never heard of people getting no food, so let me talk to my supervisor to see who we should talk to. Where to you live?"

"Ten miles east of Brewton, Alabama."

"Okay, I'll be back in just a minute. Please stay on the line."

Amber quickly filled out the details she knew on a green card and approached Mr. Quinn. He looked annoyed that she was back already.

"I thought I told you I would give you information on your friend after shift."

"Yes, Mr. Quinn. This is something different - I have someone on the line who has never received any food – no airdrops and no food left when the phone line was put in."

"That's impossible. All the reports say a full pallet is left with every phone put in."

"I had a call last week saying each person in that neighborhood only got five MREs each. That was Georgia. This lady is in Alabama. She's crying and says her children will barely move because they are so hungry."

"Give me the card – I'll be right back."

Amber watched Mr. Quinn walk into the room where the cards were delivered at the end of each shift. He closed the door behind him, but she could hear his muffled voice through it and strained to make out the words, but she couldn't. He came out rather quickly and his face had turned red.

"Tell her there will be an airdrop tomorrow. And if there is not, tell her to call back."

Amber went back to the phone and told the lady the information. She cried and said thank you before hanging up. Amber had about thirty seconds to recover before the phone rang again. Luckily, it was just about a rash. She could deal with medical and electrical issues easily enough, but she had trouble dealing with people who were hungry. Especially right before she was to head to lunch where there was more food than she could ever eat.

At lunch, Natasha noticed Amber was being rather quiet. She told her about the phone call and Natasha said she had a call that said they were going to run out of food in a week. They had been calling from Louisiana. They said the same thing about getting no food when the phone was installed, too. They knew from the briefing updates that the Southern states had just been helped out in the last two months with phone installation, but they had been getting more airdrops since they had waited so long.

"Something isn't adding up. Maybe we should start our own list of these phone calls," Natasha said. Amber took a notebook out of her bag and they started jotting down notes about what had been mentioned about food and airdrops in their calls in the last few days. They agreed to add to it and look harder at it on their next day off.

Amber found a note on her desk when she returned from lunch. It read: Alex McCarthy, CP8527, auto detail.

She looked up and made eye contact with Mr. Quinn. She smiled at him and he nodded back at her before she sat down. She could finally contact her friend! She wished she hadn't waited to long to figure out how to contact him. She sat by herself at dinner so she could write him a letter and then get it to the message center after her shift. She just knew he would write back soon. She wondered if they could meet up if they had the same day off. She went to bed smiling that night.

Amber checked for a message at every mealtime. After two days, the woman at the desk would make eye contact with Amber while she was in line and just nod her head no. Amber would then leave. The morning of her next day off, she got in line at the message center before breakfast. This time, when the woman caught her eye, she nodded yes and smiled. Amber smiled back. She only had to wait for two people to finish, but it felt like an eternity.

"I have a letter for you, Amber Birch," the woman said, handing the envelope to her.

"Thank you so much!" Amber replied and quickly moved out of the line and opened up the letter.

> *Dear Amber,*
>
> *Hi! I hope you're doing well! I wasn't happy about being assigned to the vehicle detail at first, but it's actually quite an interesting job and I get to go out and travel some.*
>
> *I had asked around when I first got assigned if there was a way to contact you and nobody I asked knew. I was so glad to get a letter from you. The person who delivered it to the auto detail came when I was there so I asked how I could send a reply. There's a mailroom right around the corner from the office! Guess no one else I work with has anyone they want to get in touch with.*
>
> *I haven't been able to talk to my parents yet. I've been able to call your house a few times, but no one answered. Have you been able to call home?*
>
> *It took a while to reply because I was out in Tennessee. My boss brought me the message the next day. I've gotten a mechanic's license and they send us out to repair government trucks or help towns for a week getting cars working again. There's still not a lot of working gas stations, but I think next year will be big for getting*

services back up.

Tell me more about the phone calls you get. I don't know if there's a way we can meet. My schedule is a day shift with three days on and one day off, but when we travel we don't get time off. When we return, we get one day off per week we've been gone and then our schedule starts over again.

Our dorms are above ground and it sounds like you're in the underground area. Is it hard not seeing the outside? We have a cafeteria and store, too. There's an outside and inside rec area, too. Rumor is you guys have a swimming pool and bowling alley. Is that true?

Time to hit the rack. The line of cars to work on tomorrow is long.

Write back soon!
Alex

Amber tucked the letter into her tote bag and headed to breakfast. Natasha and Jessie were there and she told them the good news as soon as she sat down.

"I bet you feel better knowing where he is," Natasha said.

"I sure do," Amber said.

"So, is Alex your boyfriend?" Jessie asked. Amber looked at her and almost spit out her orange juice.

"Um, no, not really. Um, we're just really good friends," Amber said, her cheeks getting hot. She saw Jessie and Natasha exchange glances. Alex was her best friend and while she had no plans to date anyone until college, she found herself thinking about the kiss on her forehead a lot. She wasn't up for discussing this with people she barely knew, though.

"Um, hey, want to play Monopoly after this?" she asked, changing the topic. The other girls laughed but let the topic drop.

They were setting up the game board when two boys approached them, but just stood there. Amber looked up and saw one of the boys was Drew, but he was using a cane. She was sure he hadn't had one the other morning.

"Can we help you?" Jessie finally said.

"Um, we usually play Monopoly in the mornings," the boy with Drew said. He had wire glasses and was not much taller than Amber's little brother.

"Well, so do we, but we've never seen you here," Natasha said. Amber could sense she was getting ready to argue with them.

"Our schedules just got changed," Drew said. "This is our day off now. Hey, wait; you're that new girl I helped, right? Angela?"

"It's Amber. You're Drew, right? Well, how about we all play?" Amber said.

"I don't mind playing with some more people. Do you, Scott?"

"I don't if they don't mind losing," he said, laughing.

The boys made their way to the other end of the table. Drew sat by Amber and the Scott sat by Jessie. Natasha was at the end. Amber asked where Drew and Scott worked.

"We work on the phone lines."

"Natasha and I do, too," Amber said. "Jessie here works in the cafeteria and only joins us occasionally." While the boys were making sure their chairs were several inches apart from the girls, Amber could see them start to relax.

"Have you been here long?" Natasha said.

"We came three months after the power went out," Scott said. "Our families were at Virginia Beach together for spring break when it happened. We lived on the other side of Virginia. All of us decided to come work instead of trying to make it home."

"So, your whole family is here?" Amber asked.

"It's just us and our parents," Drew said. "This is kind of weird, but both our dads are doctors and our moms are nurses and they all work at the same hospital. Our parents are helping at Walter Reed. Our moms have come to see us twice, but they work longer shifts than us."

"That is kind of weird, but really cool, too," Jessie said.

"Yeah, it is what it is. So, can I be the shoe?" Scott asked. They laughed and started playing.

After dinner, Amber and Natasha went over the phone calls they had gotten about food. They caught Jessie up with what the calls had been about.

"That's seven calls total in the past week," Amber said

after she finished jotting down Natasha's calls.

"We should ask those guys if they've gotten any calls about it," Natasha said.

"I can keep my ears open when I'm out in the cafeteria wiping down tables. If I hear anything, I'll send you a message through the message center in case I don't see you again for a while."

"Thanks, Jessie. I hope it's just a weird fluke," Natasha said.

"It's got to be," Amber said. "But it wouldn't hurt to pay attention and make sure."

Amber found another mean note from her roommate on the bathroom mirror that night. There had been one every night since Marissa had confronted her in the hallway. This one told her to shower because she made the room stink. Amber crumpled it up and put it in the trashcan like she had done with all the others. Marissa sometimes moved her things around, but never damaged anything and while the notes were mean, they weren't threatening. Amber didn't think there was anything anyone could do about them, so she kept quiet. She didn't even tell Natasha about it.

A few days later, on the next day off, Scott and Drew joined Amber and Natasha at breakfast. Natasha wasted no time telling them about the phone calls they had gotten the week before.

"I haven't had any calls like that," Drew said. "With winter hitting, I'm getting a lot of calls for directions to the closest mall or military base."

"My first day on the job, I did get a weird phone call that might have been about this," Scott said. "A man asked when their food was coming, but when I started to ask him questions, the call dropped. That's the only one I've had, though."

"I'll add Scott's call to our notes," Amber said. "I didn't get any calls this week "

"Neither did I," Natasha said.

"Let's hope none of us do any more," Scott said. "I really hate thinking about people going hungry."

When they left to walk to the break room to play another game of Monopoly, Amber ended up walking beside Drew.

"Can I ask why you use a cane?" she said.

"Sure," he replied, tapping it on the wall. "I have juvenile arthritis. Some days are good and I don't need it, but some days, my legs hurt and using the cane helps."

"How long have you had it?"

"Since I was about 11. I played a lot of sports up until then. One day, my left leg just started aching. It took them several months to figure out what it was. I try to take as little medicine for it as possible."

"I'm sorry," Amber said.

"It's okay. I'm still able to do some sports on my good days. It's actually been nice to be here away from my parents. They tend to hover and make a big deal. Most people around here don't care as long as I'm doing my job," he said, turning to smile at her.

"Well, if there's ever anything I can do to help on a bad day, let me know," she said.

"Thanks, Amber." He put a hand on her shoulder but then quickly removed it as they turned into the break room.

CHAPTER THIRTEEN

Now that Amber had connected with Alex, she was eager to get a call home to her parents. She started making a habit of checking the phone call list near the message center right when her last shift of the workweek ended. It had been more than a month now since she'd left home. She had sent two letters home but had not received any response.

"Yes!" she said as she saw her number was up for tomorrow. She would be able to call home at the end of the day. Her family should definitely be home at 7 p.m. She had been worried she'd get a time slot when her family would all be out of the house working. When she turned to head back to go to dinner, she noticed a few people staring at her. She must have been louder than she thought. She just smiled and headed to the cafeteria.

Amber had trouble concentrating that next day waiting for her phone call slot. She lost the game of Monopoly by a huge margin and barely managed to teach her sewing class. It was more a lesson of what not to do as she sewed her pieces of fabric together right side out instead of right side together. She tried reading but ended up staring at the wall for the most part. During breakfast and lunch, her friends kept trying to bring her into the conversation, but she kept thinking about all the things she wanted to talk to her parents about.

She picked up a sandwich to go for dinner so she could wait by the phone until it was her turn. Finally, it was time to call home. The phone only rang twice before it was answered.

"Hello?"

"Mom, it's Amber!"

"Amber! Jack – come here! It's Amber! How are you?"

"I'm good, Mom. It's busy here. I'm answering phone calls and helping people troubleshoot all kinds of problems."

"Is Alex doing that, too?"

"No, but he's at the same location working on cars. We've been able to write letters to each other, but I haven't seen him since they separated us for quarantine."

"Quarantine?"

"I know. But they had to make sure we weren't sick after all that time without power. We're all stuck in a building, so they have to keep us healthy. It might even be underground."

"Honey, you don't sound happy. I just talked to Justine yesterday and they haven't heard anything from Alex. We were both getting pretty worried about you two."

"I'm just tired. I work some pretty long days. There's so much noise with electricity running and people working round the clock. There's lots of food, though. Tell Christopher I had chocolate chip cookies and ice cream yesterday. Oh, and I found out what the actual date is - Nov. 12. Make sure to tell Ivy and Veronica."

"Sure, honey. Let me put Dad on the line."

"Amber?" Dad asked.

"It's me, Dad. How are you?"

"Good. Your Mom wants me to tell you that Christopher is working at the farm full-time now. Mr. Speer fell last week and can't do everything that needs to be done. He's not doing so well at his age anyway."

"That's good that Christopher can help him. I was just telling Mom to tell him I had chocolate chip cookies and ice cream yesterday. Is this still the only phone around?"

"It is and you're the only call we've gotten on it. The only sign we've seen of the government since you left is another airdrop. We're going to need it for the winter, I think, unless they show up soon to connect the power. Is there any number we can call to reach you if we need to tell you anything?"

"Oh, yes, there is. I almost forgot. You call (202) 557-3321 and ask to send a message to AF3274. I tried calling twice before, but it was during the day. I'll see if there's a way I can request evening time slots."

She repeated the contact information for them three times and told them about the letters she had sent so they could look out for them. They told her that Mr. Sanders came back a few weeks ago. They had made him do manual labor as a punishment for stealing and then sent him home. Her dad noted that he seemed a bit more withdrawn, but did help out in the neighborhood. When they were done talking, it was hard to say goodbye. She wanted to listen to their voices for hours. She could hear how much they missed her. After she hung up, she realized how much she had been looking forward to hearing her brother's voice, too. He could always lighten her spirits, even if most times it was in an annoying manner.

The one thing she didn't tell her parents was the problems her roommate was giving her. It seemed like Marissa was trying her best to get Amber to request a room change. She still moved Amber's belongings around and left notes, but now she also hid her toothbrush and messed up her just-made bed. Marissa would then also leave notes telling Amber to clean up her mess – the mess Marissa had created. It was infuriating at times, but Amber didn't want to deal with it. She decided to keep her most precious belongings with her at all times and tuck her toothbrush away where Marissa wouldn't find it. She stopped making her bed and made neat piles of her clothes instead of hanging them up. If her side was already a little messy, then Marissa couldn't really mess it up much more. Marissa had then started leaving her stuff alone, but still left a note every single day.

A week later, a new policy was implemented at work where they had to fill out an extra card for every call, but this one was green instead of white. At the end of each phone call, she had to try and ask the caller to complete a survey. It was only a few questions long, but she noticed it was the same questions she was asked at one of the testing stations.

Can I get an exact address of your location?

How many people are alive in your house? Neighborhood?

Have you had access to any airdrops? How many? When?

How many people do you know have died since the power went out?

The cards were turned in at the end of the shift to their supervisor, which was almost always Mr. Quinn or Mr. Fray. One day, she had stood up to quickly get a bottle of water from the back of the room and saw Mr. Fray open the door that led to the room next door with the cards and give them to a person in that room. There were about four rows of tables with computers on them and people typing away. She also glanced at maps on the walls with different colored pushpins all over. She guessed they were analyzing the information on the note cards. Mr. Fray shut the door again before she could find her home area on the map. Now that would be an interesting place to work, she thought.

Even though Mr. Quinn was moody, Amber liked when he was working with them more than Mr. Fray. Mr. Fray was completely bald and never smiled. While Mr. Quinn tended to be working on a computer when he was in the room, Mr. Fray just sat at the desk with his arms crossed, watching them. He didn't say a single word more than necessary when anyone talked to him.

On their next day off, Amber and her friends finally met in the cafeteria for breakfast. They had tried talking to each other when they passed in the hall or at meals, but on workdays, their time was almost completely tied up. None of them woke up in time to enjoy breakfast most workdays – they all did the same kind of dash and grab Amber had done her first day of training. They had been on different lunch shifts this week, too. They all purposely moved at a much slower pace on their days off.

"What do you think they're doing with all the green cards?" Drew asked at breakfast.

"I got a glimpse of the room they're taking them to and it looks like they're trying to analyze the data," Amber said.

"There's maps with pushpins all over them."

"I had a hysteric phone call this week and the lady was asking what to do because her children were starving," Natasha. "She hadn't had an airdrop in months she said – and she lived in Georgia. I asked if they gave food when the trucks came to put in the phone and she said each family got only five MRE packets. I walked her through some wild edibles, but had to suggest she get to the closest mall, which was thirty-five miles away."

"That's awful! Didn't they say last week that there were twenty-five airdrops in the Southern States at the last update briefing? Hopefully they sent food to that location based on the green card you turned in," Scott said.

"I hope so, too," Amber said. "I'd hate to think they possibly made the green cards to help with this. They've been doing food drops for, what, close to two years now? They have to have some kind of system."

"I doubt they made the cards just for this," Drew said.

"You're probably right," Amber replied. "Maybe I should lay off the Clancy books for a while." Scott laughed, but Natasha and Drew just looked at each other and shrugged.

"Tom Clancy? The guy who writes the government conspiracy thriller books?" Amber asked. "Don't you guys read?"

"Um, yes, but not his books yet," Natasha said.

"I'll loan you one. And then Drew can read it after you," Scott said.

The next week, Amber had a call each day about food. Most people had gone at least two months without an airdrop. She thought to ask one woman who called for directions to a mall why she was going and she said it was because the food was running low in her neighborhood and she didn't want her children to be hungry. She said they had been regular until last month and then they just stopped. She counted that as her fifth food call for the week. She was anxious to see how many her friends had gotten that week.

"I had three calls about food this week," Scott said before taking a bite of his bagel.

"I had five," Amber said. "Where were yours from?" She had a notepad and pen ready to go by her coffee mug.

"Two were from Mississippi – Tupelo and near Jackson. The other one was from Louisiana. I couldn't understand the city name. The lady talking had a heavy Creole accent."

"So, that's eight total for this week," Amber said. She had already written down the information from her calls and was adding Scott's calls.

"It seems like they're all in the South," Drew said. "I didn't get any calls."

"I got one this week," Natasha said. "Niceville, Florida.

"I heard someone talking about one this week," Jessie piped in. "He said he had a call from Mississippi scamming for more food."

"Well, it seems like something is not going right," Scott said. "The briefing is in about thirty minutes. I wonder if they'll mention it at all."

"They always seem to just report on the positive things," Amber said. "I think we need to see what they say first and then decide what to do. If anything, Mr. Quinn seemed quite helpful when I told him about the very first call I got."

They finished their breakfast and decided to meet in the computer room after the briefing. They would see if they could find anything on the Internet about food possibly not being delivered. Then, they would play Monopoly.

Amber made a quick run to the message center before heading to the briefing. She wanted to see if Alex had replied to her last letter yet. Their correspondence was erratic, but she usually got a letter every two to three weeks. She didn't have any messages, though. She made it back to the briefing just in time, but had to take a seat in the back instead of with her friends.

The man up front on the stage was in a suit and tie, something she only saw a person wearing at the briefing. Everyone else she had encountered wore the standard khakis and polos with tennis shoes. She wondered why he always wore a suit and guessed it was to look more professional.

"I want to start off with our phone connection tally. We are up to 68 percent of neighborhoods being connected.

There is still work to be done in the Deep South, the more mountainous terrain and the rural areas. Food deliveries have been ramped up now that factories on both the East and West coasts are fully operational. Remember a lot of the factories had to be built from the ground up to replace damaged systems and food had to imported from other countries.

"We have been made aware that while waiting for the new round of shipments, some places in the South did not receive full rations. Those rations are being delivered this week.

"Power lines are getting close to being fully laid down. We estimate that power will be restored to more than half of the country by the spring. A majority of the states on the coasts have power restored."

Several people clapped and shouted, including Amber. Life would return to "normal" soon, she hoped.

"It's amazing how much our life depends on power," Amber whispered to herself.

"Do you believe all that?" she heard a voice behind her. Before she could turn around, another voice answered. "I don't know. I hope so. There were so many calls this week from hungry people."

She recognized the second voice as Mr. Quinn. She decided not to turn around so she could listen in, but the two men walked away.

Amber waited for her friends to walk up the auditorium stairs towards her to see if they still wanted to walk together to the lounge. They didn't talk until they got into the room and settled into one of the computer workrooms that had a door. Then, Amber told them what she had heard.

"It sounds like they've taken care of the problem," Natasha said. "What do you think, Drew?"

"It does sound like it. Let me do a quick search anyway. It probably won't take long if you guys want to go set up the board."

Drew came out shortly after they got the board set up.

"There's nothing out there," he said. "I don't think most places even have Internet to report anything. The newspapers are reporting exactly what we're hearing at the briefings.

They're also reporting that a lot of the normal harvest in the Midwest this year was lost to insects and disease."

"So, they're trusting the government for the correct information," Scott said. "Laziness."

"It would be weird to be living out on the coasts, knowing that the most of the country is back in the Dark Ages. Do any of them come out to work here?" Amber asked.

"They don't," Natasha said. "I asked about that during my introductory briefing and was told they want to keep their lives as normal as possible. They are allowing teenagers to work at 14 now where there's power if they're still in school so they have more factory workers. They want some of the country still going to high school and college to keep our future stable."

"That makes sense," Amber said. They were all going to attend their first GED class in a few weeks. They all wanted to get their high school diploma equivalencies completed as soon as they could. They could take the test after just ten weeks. After lunch she had her sewing class and then she hoped to read the rest of the day.

Before reading later that afternoon, she went to see what was new on the bulletin board in the lounge. She was shocked to find a full page with her name in big block letters with the words slob, messy, be considerate, know your place, hoarder, sloppy written beside it. She tore it off the board and threw it in the trash. It had to be Marissa. She debated leaving a similar note back to Marissa, but couldn't make herself do it. She had heard Marissa might leave at the end of the year. If she could just get through a few more months, surely the next roommate wouldn't be this mean.

She stopped by the message center before heading to her room for the night and was so happy to have a letter from Alex. He told her all about his latest trip to the panhandle of Florida.

Amber was just putting the letter back in the envelope when she reached her room. As she went to open the door, her roommate came out at the exact moment and walked right into her.

"Oh, it's you. Well, good. I was going to leave you a

note, but this will save me the time," Marissa said. "I'm leaving in two days. My time is up and I'm heading to California for school. Make sure you don't have any of my stuff tucked away anywhere."

"Good luck," Amber said as Marissa started to walk away. "Wait – will I get a new roommate?"

"Probably. I don't know. Bye."

Amber sighed and forced herself to not say anything mean in reply. She'd have to remember to ask someone tomorrow how the new roommate assignments worked. She smiled as she walked into her room. The day had been full of good news. It was just a few days until her birthday and Marissa leaving was just the present she wanted. She got ready for bed and then started a letter back to Alex, but fell asleep before finishing it.

CHAPTER FOURTEEN

Amber asked Natasha what she knew about roommate assignments at breakfast before work the next day. Natasha said she'd had three different roommates and it was usually less than a week until the new roommate showed up, but there was never any say in who was assigned to what room. Amber had three quiet weeks with no roommate and no food calls for her or her friends and then one day there were clothes scattered about the room. It did make the small space seem even more crowded. Amber decided to leave her new roommate a note, but a much nicer one than Marissa had left her. She welcomed her and explained that sharing a room was easier if they both kept things neat, that way it could feel like their own room when they were in it. She asked where she was from and said she would try to stop by early one day after her shift so they could meet in person. She put the note on the bathroom sink and then left for her shift.

When she came back to the room that night, she saw a blond girl about her height leaving the room. She ran up to her.

"Hi! I'm Amber, your roommate," she said as she caught up to the girl.

"Oh, hi. I was hoping I'd see you soon. I have so many questions ..." the girl said.

"I remember feeling like that. You'll get it all figured out soon. What's your name?"

"I'm Lillian. I'm from a small town in Alabama, near the Florida border."

"I'm from North Carolina."

"Neat. We went to Charleston, South Carolina, for vacation the year before the power went out."

"I've been there a few times, but we never got down to Florida. We had been thinking of it for a senior year trip for me, but now I'm here."

Lillian looked down the hall anxiously.

"I have to go if I want to eat before work. But, one quick question - do you know how to contact home? I want to make sure we finally got the food we were promised."

"Food?"

"We went months without food and they said if we volunteered, our town would get extra portions, but they would have to deliver them later. A few of us decided to go, but there were doubts the food would ever come. I don't want to stay if my family is starving. So many people didn't make it this winter. We've had too much rain over the summer and didn't get much from our gardens."

Amber put a hand on Lillian's shoulder. She could see the tears starting to form in Lillian's eyes.

"There's a way to call on your day off, but for something like this, you may want to try your supervisor. I'll leave you a note with more details for your day off, though."

"Thanks. I really appreciate it. I better go. Hopefully we'll run into each other soon."

"I hope so, too."

Amber went into her room and saw the lights were already starting to dim. She didn't have time to go tell the others what she just learned about the food. Could there still be places waiting for food after all this time? Were the reports true or were they being lied to? It took her a long time to fall asleep. She could still remember what it felt like to be hungry, but that was a hunger with smaller portions of food, not with no food at all.

"Hello, this is Amber at AmVoc. How may I help you?"

"It fell on my roof! You all better come fix it!"

"What fell on your roof, ma'am?"

"The food! The entire food bundle fell on my roof and landed in my son's bedroom! You guys are lucky he wasn't in there. We need it fixed. It's already cold at night. We've had to stay at a neighbor's."

"Let me get down your details so we can report this. Where do you live?"

"In Owenton, Kentucky – about thirty minutes from Cincinnati."

"Was anyone hurt?"

"No, thank God."

"Were you able to save the food?"

"It's still up in my house. We have plenty to go around. We get about three drops a week."

"Three a week?"

"Yep. They didn't even stop after we got the power back on."

"Okay. Would you like to hold or have someone call you back?"

"Call me back. I have to go get some laundry done. But they better come fix it quick!"

Amber finished filling out the report on the call and jotted down a few details in her small notebook. She then took the card up to Mr. Fray.

"Mr. Fray, I haven't dealt with this situation before – an MRE drop hit a house." She handed him the card. "It's in Kentucky."

He looked up at her and then looked back at the card.

"That is a new one. I wonder if it was an accidental release," Mr. Fray said. He got up to go to the data room.

"There's one other thing. I didn't put on the card, but I thought you would want to know. The woman said they get three food drops a week there."

"Three? A week? Are you sure you heard right? Areas are supposed to get one or maybe two a month."

"I'm sure, sir. I asked her twice."

"Thank you, Amber. I'll go report this so we can get a

repair crew out there. I'm sure there's some kind of process for this."

When she came back from lunch the next day, there was a note on her desk asking her to see Mr. Quinn. As she approached, he stood up and gestured for her to follow him. He went through a door that she had always assumed was the supervisor break room. She looked around as he closed the door. It was a normal conference room with several large white boards on the walls. They were all blank.

"Have a seat, Amber," Mr. Quinn said. She picked a chair and then he sat down right next to her.

"I think you might be able to help us out with something. We're not quite sure how yet, but a few of us are starting an investigation into the possibility of food drops being rerouted."

"Rerouted?"

"Yes, we're getting data that shows food drops aren't being delivered where they're supposed to. Your call today was the first one we've had that helps support the idea that some places might be getting more than their fair share."

"How could that happen? Why?"

"That's what we've got to find out. Would you like to help?"

She agreed to what he proposed and told her what her and her friends were already tracking.

When Amber got to her room, Lillian had already left. She looked at the time and realized she had almost an hour before the lights started dimming. She decided to write a note to leave Lillian and write another letter back to Alex. She needed to know Lillian's work schedule. If both of their off days matched up, they could talk on those days. She needed to know if Lillian's area had ever received any food or airdrops. How many people lived where she lived? How many people had died? Did she ever make the call to see if her neighborhood had gotten any food? She tried to limit the questions, but she filled up an entire sheet. She propped it up behind the sink and then washed her face, brushed her teeth and changed into pajamas. She was getting tired and even though she wanted to write Alex back, she thought it might have to wait until tomorrow. She had received two more letters from him after writing him back after the first letter. She confirmed with her friends that there was no swimming pool or bowling alley in her area. There was a workout room, though, that she hadn't known about before. He sounded like he enjoyed his work. The travel made up for being put on car duty. They would keep trying to see if their schedules ever matched for days off. Alex said he would keep track and if he ever had the same day off as her, he would try to come visit. She at least worked during the day and slept at night, if the clocks were right. Neither of them knew if a visit was even possible, but Alex said he'd find a way if he could. She read his letters over and then tucked them in her bag so she could write him back tomorrow.

The lights started dimming just as she started to get into bed. Her mind wandered back to the food problem. Why would someone not deliver food? Did they run out? Or was it going somewhere else? Who could be doing it?

Amber had to wait until her next day off to talk to her friends about what Mr. Quinn proposed. She had asked him if they could help and he said they could as long as they kept what they were doing quiet. He especially liked the idea of Jessie listening in the cafeteria area. She first told them about her new roommate and then about Mr. Quinn's investigation.

"How would we be helping him?" Scott asked.

"He wants us to hold onto any green cards that deal with food calls and hand them off only to him or Mr. Fray at the end of the day instead of putting them in the filing container. He said we could make copies for ourselves and wanted us to keep our own records. He might ask to look at them occasionally."

"He can't be the one leading the investigation, can he?" Drew asked.

"No, he mentioned he and Mr. Fray were working with three other supervisors who had been picked by the government's Office of Special Investigations. They don't know if the problem is originating here, at the warehouses or in the military chain."

"I'm in," Jessie said. "I'll be more focused now on seeing what I can hear when people are in here eating."

"Speaking of that, maybe we shouldn't talk about it in here," Natasha said.

"Oh, good point," Amber replied.

"What if we started a new book club that only includes us?" Natasha suggested. "We just won't advertise it, but we can meet in one of the small study rooms, and then we have a reason to be meeting up where no one can hear us."

"I'm going to buy us each a copy of something at the store real quick and bring it to the lounge," Scott said. "Let's meet there after the update briefing."

Amber nodded. "Good idea."

"I'll go with you, Scott," Natasha said and got up to leave. She paused as she stood and whispered, "We probably shouldn't sit together in the update briefing anymore either."

Amber and Drew glanced at each other as Natasha and Scott walked away.

"Do you ever think ..." Drew asked.

"Really? Those two?" Amber giggled. "I don't know if many people think about any type of romantic relationship in this place. We barely have time to take care of ourselves here."

"True," Drew said. "Sorry to have to leave you, but I have to go try and get a phone call in to my parents before the briefing. I can only call when I'm off on a Sunday as one of them always has that day off at the hospital."

"Okay. See you later," Amber said. As she watched Drew walk away, she realized there were still a lot of her friends' lives she didn't know about. They didn't talk about home much, so she didn't know about their parents or siblings, except where they were from. It was easier, she guessed, to not think about what people at home might be dealing with while they had electricity, running water and lots of food. Amber was hoping she'd be picked for another call home soon. She needed to know how her family was doing now that it was winter.

The update briefing was very short that day and there was no mention of food drops at all. It made Amber wonder if more than just them and the few supervisors knew about the investigation. She wondered if Alex would know anything about it from his traveling around. She decided to send him a quick letter asking about it before meeting up with her friends. She wouldn't tell them about asking him unless he had any information.

Amber, Natasha, Scott, Drew and Jessie spent two full hours sharing the calls they had gotten that week, reviewing their own data and coming up with how they were going to help Mr. Quinn track the data. Jessie was able to sketch up a picture of the U.S. in Amber's notebook and they could put dots where they had received calls. Amber noted the call about the extra food with a square.

"I wish we could have access to all the data," Natasha said.

"Me, too, but if this is just a sampling, there's a lot of places where people aren't getting enough food," Amber said.

"Do you think people missing one month's food drop is that big of a deal?" Drew asked. "We always had enough food without them."

"We just barely did with the drops and our gardens were great. There are places where gardens don't work well or they might not grow well," Amber said.

"If the bigger harvests didn't do well this summer, than a lot of the small ones probably didn't either," Scott added.

"No one should be going hungry," Natasha said, gritting her teeth. No one said anything for a few seconds. Amber put her hand on Natasha's arm.

"That's what we're going to help with."

CHAPTER FIFTEEN

Just two weeks later, Amber got to call home again. Her call was scheduled for 2 p.m., but she managed to pay someone for a trade who had parents on the West Coast and needed to call them earlier in the day.

"Hello?" Amber heard Christopher answer.

"Christopher! Hi, it's Amber."

"Amber, how are you?"

"I'm doing good. Are you not at the Speers' farm anymore?"

"I just go over during the day a few times a week now. Not much to do except help with the animals, fix things and keep the tools in good shape."

"How has the winter been?"

"It's been mild so far, thank goodness. The gardens lasted until early November. We've seen deer closer than last winter, too, which will help with food."

"Are Mom and Dad there?"

"Yes, they're hovering right behind me." Amber and Christopher both laughed at that.

"So good to hear your voice, " Amber said, choking up a little.

"You, too, Sis." Amber heard the shuffling as the phone was handed off.

"Oh, Amber, what a nice surprise. Happy late birthday, dear," her mother said.

"Thank you, Mom."

"Did you do anything to celebrate?"

"Not really, but I did get an extra piece of cake for myself at the cafeteria that night. Are you guys doing okay? Have enough food?"

"Yes, it's such a more mild winter. We get an airdrop nearby about every four to six weeks. We see them drop all around the area some days."

"Good. I'm so glad. And next winter you should have power!"

Her mother sighed.

"You sound good, dear. Your father is dying to talk to you, too."

Amber told her father about the GED classes and how she was teaching a sewing class.

"You're making some friends, too, right?" he asked.

"Yes, some good ones actually. Drew and Scott have parents working at the hospital at Walter Reed. Natasha came from Pennsylvania."

"Sound like interesting people. We actually had two teenagers come to the neighborhood a few weeks ago. They're living with the Reeds. They're twin brothers and their parents had both passed away – one a year ago from diabetes and the other a few weeks ago from a heart attack. They didn't know what to do when their food ran low, so they started walking to find someone to help them. They had lived on old family farm about 20 miles north of us, but had no neighbors for miles since they rented out some of the land to farmers."

"That's sad. I bet they would love to work out here," Amber suggested.

"We'll see what they want to do when the workers get back this way again. It should be soon," he said.

"My time is about up, Dad. I love you."

"Love you, too. Here's mom again."

"I love you, Amber. Take care of yourself!"

"I will, Mom. I love you, too!"

Amber quickly hung up the phone before she started crying. She was so busy most of the time that she didn't realize how homesick she was. Life was harder there, but it had been with her family. She wiped her eyes and then stepped out of the phone room. She found a corner in the break room and took out the photo of her family from her bag and looked at them for a while, letting a few more tears fall. Then, she dried the tears, put the photo away and decided to write a long letter to Alex telling him all that her family had told her. He had written her back that past week and said he hadn't been anywhere where people were desperate for food at all. In fact, almost everywhere they went the people seemed very well fed.

Amber groaned inwardly as she saw Mr. Fray sitting at the supervisor desk later that week. She saw a note on her desk as she put her bag down that asked her to go up and see him. She'd rarely talked to him one on one. It had to be something about the investigation.

When he saw her walk toward him, he started heading to the supervisor break room, just like Mr. Quinn had done. He opened the door and let her go in first. She could feel the eyes of some of the other teens watching them. He started talking as soon as the door closed, not even giving her time to sit down.

"Amber Birch, right?" She nodded. "I just needed to tell you that the investigation into the food drops is over and closed. We won't need your help anymore. Please tell your friends and make sure they keep quiet about the whole thing."

He moved to the door, but Amber said, "Wait!"

"What?"

"What happened? Why were people not getting food drops?"

"It was a glitch in the system. It's happened once before. They've fixed it." He opened the door and waited for her to walk out. She had more questions, but knew he wasn't going to say any more about the subject.

Later, at the end of their shift, Amber saw Natasha start to walk up to Mr. Fray's desk. She quickly moved over to her and whispered to just put the card in the basket. Natasha raised her eyebrow and Amber said she'd explain the next day at "book club."

"That's all he said?" Scott said with a scowl. "A system glitch?"

"Yep. Then he opened the door so I couldn't ask any more questions," Amber said.

"I guess it could have been," Drew said. "My new roommate works in the data room. I just found that out yesterday. I can see what he's heard."

"We have to make sure he won't tell anyone else we're asking about it, though," Amber said.

"I'll say it's a question from my supervisor. If he says he's heard about the glitch, then I'd say our job is done," Drew said.

"I'd still like to keep track of any calls about food we still get. I really want to make sure it's fixed," Natasha said.

"Not a bad idea," Amber agreed.

"Sure, it couldn't hurt anything," Scott said. "But, maybe now we can relax a bit more."

Three days later, Natasha had lunch at the same time as Amber.

"I had dinner with Scott last night," she started with a smile. "He said Drew's roommate was told about the glitch problem, too. Turns out everyone working in the data room knew about the food issue and were very concerned. They actually had to tally the data by hand for the past week while the system was getting fixed."

"That's good news then," Amber said, feeling relieved that the problem was solved.

"It is. It sounds very believable," she said. "I'm still going to keep my ears open, but I already don't feel as worried."

They both got ice cream for dessert to celebrate. Amber considered signing up for some Spanish tutoring now that she'd have a bit more free time on her days off. She had taken two years of Spanish at school and still thought it would be a handy language for an elementary teacher to know.

Amber's time at AmVoc was passing by quickly. She enjoyed

having a routine, but she was still tired most of the time. The work days tended to be long and blended together, so she made sure her day off was as relaxing as it could be. It usually involved a board game or two with Natasha, Drew and Scott, reading, teaching a sewing class and not rushing through meals. They only got a phone call about food once every few weeks between the four of them and it was usually because a food drop was just a few days late. Jessie hadn't heard anything in the cafeteria. Drew started joining her for Spanish lessons and Jessie joined Amber's sewing class on her day off. She didn't know anything about sewing, but was making good progress on a simple tote bag.

Starting the end of March, they were allowed to sign up for half-day trips on their days off. They would get to go to some hiking trails located near the complex, but nowhere outside the complex fence. Amber had been so excited when she first heard about the signups. She couldn't wait to go outside.

"Did we forget to tell her about these?" Jessie asked Natasha after seeing Amber's reaction after they were announced at an update briefing. They had started sitting by each other again after the food issue was resolved.

"I guess so," Natasha said. "I think they stopped just a few weeks before she got here."

They told her they'd get a sack lunch from the cafeteria and meet up with a supervisor who would lead them through the hallways up to the parking garage. Then, a van would take them on a 15-20 minute ride outside and to a large park shelter. They could eat at the picnic tables and then walk on the trails until close to dinnertime.

"I would have been counting down the days if I'd have known. Hey, do other workers from other places in the complex get to go, too?"

"Yes, they do. Between you and me, the guys in the labor areas are much hotter than the ones they put down here," Jessie said. Natasha and Amber laughed.

"This is the best news ever," Amber smiled. "Let's go sign up and then I'll write Alex and see if he can join us."

Two weeks later, Amber was hoping Alex would be able to show up. She had written him about it and he said he'd try his hardest, but had no control over when they sent him out on repair trips, which had been more frequent lately.

When they got out of the van at the picnic shelter, Amber started looking all around, seeing if she could find Alex. There were only about 10 other teens in the area and she didn't see him. Her friends persuaded her to sit down and start eating with them, and she caved, already feeling disappointed. They were almost done eating when someone sat down across from her, sitting next to Natasha.

"Mind if I join in?" It was Alex! Amber jumped up and he came over and hugged her. When she moved to release him, he held her at arm's length for a few seconds and looked at her before letting her go. She felt a blush hit her cheeks, but then dismissed it. It had just been so long since she'd seen him.

"So, I make you speechless now?" he said, sitting down and opening his lunch.

"I just, well, you weren't here when we got here and I guessed you couldn't come," she replied. "What a great surprise!"

She looked him over for a minute. He had definitely gained weight back and had more muscles than when they parted months ago. He smiled every time he looked at her and she couldn't help but smile back.

Amber introduced Alex to her friends and they peppered him with questions about his work. When he was done eating, her friends all excused themselves and left them alone.

"Want to walk for a bit?" he asked.

"Definitely. I've been indoors since we arrived here."

"That has to be tough. I'm so glad to not only be up on the surface, but to also get to travel around."

"There's UV lighting and our rooms get really dark when it's time to sleep. I'm used to it now."

They got caught up with their lives and Amber told him all about the investigation ending and the computer glitch. The time passed quickly as they chatted. Right before they got back to the group, Alex took her hand.

"Amber, I have to tell you something. I finally connected with my parents a few weeks ago and I've decided I'm not going back home at the year mark. I'm going to stay as long as there's work to be done. I wanted to wait to tell you after I talked to them."

"Oh, that's actually great. I don't want to head home yet either. Staying here two years will get me a free ride to college. I'll probably leave after that, though."

"Well, maybe they won't need me by then either. I was worried you'd be upset and wanting to go home soon."

"I miss my family a lot, but every day I help people solve real problems. I feel like I'm where I'm supposed to be."

"Me, too," he squeezed her hand and let go. They silently walked back to the group and Alex gave her a quick hug goodbye before he headed off to get in the van that would take him back to his work area. Amber walked to her friends who were standing by a different van.

"So, that was Alex?" Natasha said with a smile. "It must be nice to get to see a friend again."

Amber just smiled and got into the van.

CHAPTER SIXTEEN

"We have great news to announce today. Two years, two months and thirteen days after the solar flare changed so much of our country, the end is in sight. All major cities will be powered within the next three months. We plan to train people from those cities to branch out from there to reconnect the communities around them. Within the year, we expect to have most of the population connected back to electricity. There are rural, outlying areas that may take longer, but our experts now say in two years or less, the entire country will be back on the grid!"

Amber couldn't help but smile and clap along with everyone in the auditorium. That was very good news.

"I do want to note that there may still be infrastructure in houses and buildings that need to be fixed, but once the power grid is active, we don't expect it to take long for people to replace or repair appliances. Companies on the coasts and around the world are working on replacement parts for cars and appliances so there will be an ample supply.

"Washington, D.C., and the surrounding area is already up and running. We are testing out all of the replacement parts and they are working great. You may share this news with family and friends that you communicate with.

"We encourage each of you to consider seeing this through until at least the power grid is fully operational. We will still honor the plan we offered you when you came, but if you stay longer, we will compensate you extra. Please talk to a Personal Matters Counselor for more details."

Amber headed straight to the Personal Matters Counselors area after the briefing, but so did a lot of people. She realized she wouldn't be able to wait in line and make it to her sewing class. She'd have to try the next day off. Her friends were all adding more activities to their days off now that they had taken and passed the GED test. They now got together for dinner and played board games afterwards until it was time to head to their rooms.

She went to the store and picked up the fabric she had ordered and then dropped it off at the sewing hobby room, a small room off the main break room that she had taken over with sewing supplies. She still had an hour, so she sat down and wrote a letter to Alex. She told him about her new roommate, the information in the briefing and asked if he knew what he would do about the extra time. She had seen him once more that summer at the afternoon outing, but they had spent that afternoon with her friends and a few of his coworkers playing lawn games. She still wanted to leave in a year and start college. She said she'd talk to a Personal Matters Counselor the next day off and would ask if there was any way they could help them meet up in person again soon. She finished the letter and hoped she could call home again soon, but after seeing the counselor so she could talk over the options with her mom.

Just as she put the letter in an envelope, the door to the room opened. Her sewing students were there. She smiled as she looked at what they were wearing – the same uniforms, but all unique with fabric flairs added here and there. Today, they were going to add patterned fabric to the hems of the khaki pants and make matching tote bags and hair bands. Sewing class was one of the highlights of her week.

"You'll never guess what I heard at lunch," Jessie said at dinner that night. "Two people were talking about a call one of them had gotten from Georgia about not getting any food for three months."

"No," Natasha said, shaking her head. "It can't happen

again."

"Maybe this is just a one-time thing," Scott said. "I haven't had any calls about it."

"Neither have I," Drew said. Amber shook her head in agreement.

"It has been a long time, but if there's been two computer glitches already, there could be a third," Natasha said. "You should tell Mr. Quinn, Amber."

"I'm sure they know from the green card on it," Amber said. Natasha glared at her. "How about we see if we get any calls ourselves this week? Then, I'll talk to him."

"That's probably the smartest thing," Scott said. "We can't verify what they said."

"Fine," Natasha said. "Thanks for telling us, Jessie."

Before they got up to leave, Amber asked them how much longer they planned to work at AmVoc.

"Are you guys considering staying longer after this morning?" she asked.

"I'd have to see what they're going to offer us," Natasha said. "I really just want to get to college. The work schedule here is tiring."

"I agree," Drew said as he yawned. "Tell us if you find out what they're offering for an extension. The line was so long all day today. I checked it three times."

Amber dropped her letter off to Alex at the mailroom after they played two games of Life and then decided to see if there was any time to speak to a Personal Matters Counselor. The doors were closed, but there was a sign up for appointments. She signed up for one early on her next day off.

She had a hard time falling asleep that night. She kept wondering what they would offer if she stayed longer. Would her parents still want her to go to college? Or would they want her to stay longer?

Amber didn't have any calls out of the ordinary the next day. Her roommate had replied to a note she had left that she'd not heard anything about people not getting food. She promised to let Amber know if she did. The few times she saw her friends, none of them had gotten any food calls either.

However, on the last day of the workweek, Amber got a distressing call.

"AmVoc citizen help line. This is Amber. How may I help you?"

"It's been a month since they left. Where is our food?"

"Where are you located?"

"Downsville, Louisiana."

"Tell me more about what happened," Amber reached for a scrap piece of paper to write down the details for herself.

"It's been over a month since they came and counted us and told us the power would be coming on soon. We sent five of our best workers with them for volunteer work and they promised us more food would be coming and it hasn't."

"Did they leave any food before they left?"

"Just one big thing of those pre-packaged meals, but that was only enough for three for each person. They said they would make sure more was coming soon. When will it be here? We haven't had much rain and nothing's grown in our gardens."

"More food should be coming. I need to take down your name, your exact location and how many people there are around you. I also have some survey questions I need to ask to help us stay informed about America's situation. I promise you someone will look into this today and get back with you soon."

Amber filled out the white and green cards and tucked the scrap piece of paper into her pocket. She'd wait until the shift was over and then talk to Mr. Quinn.

Her phone started ringing.

"AmVoc citizen help line. This is Amber. How may I help you?"

"We got these mushrooms in the back yard. Can we eat them?"

She quickly turned to the section in her binder on mushrooms and answered the call. The rest of her calls were routine calls like that one.

She waited until just about everyone had left and then went up to Mr. Quinn.

"Excuse me," she said quietly. He looked up from a report he was reading and gave her a bit of a glare.

"What, Miss Birch?"

"Sir, I think the food situation is happening again."

Mr. Quinn looked slightly taken aback and reached out for the green card she was holding. She gave it to him and stood there while he read it over.

"They said ... surely not more ..." he muttered under his breath. He stood up. "This isn't more than thirty miles from where my sister lives. I was really optimistic this was all over since you and your friends weren't giving me any more cards."

"Mr. Fray told me the investigation was over and to not turn them in anymore."

Mr. Quinn stared at her for a minute and then closed his eyes and put his hand on his forehead. "Mr. Fray must have been misinformed. The investigation is still ongoing. There was a computer glitch, but it didn't explain all the situations we had. Can you start giving us the cards again, please?"

"Yes, Mr. Quinn. My friend in the cafeteria actually heard some people talking about a call from Georgia where there was no food drops for three months."

"I will handle this right away. Thank you for letting me know." He then went to the data room. Amber headed to her room not knowing what to think. She wondered why Mr. Fray told them not to turn in the green cards anymore. Was he just misinformed? Amber swung by the phone list before heading to her room and saw her number for 4 p.m. She'd keep the time and hope someone would answer. If so, she'd be able to tell them about the details of the extension offer.

Amber had to get to her appointment with the Personal Matters Counselor before she could meet up with her friends and tell them what she learned. She hoped they'd still be at breakfast; otherwise she'd have to wait until dinner unless she could track them all down. She got ready quickly and picked out a bagel and orange juice to go from the cafeteria. She got to the Personal Matters Counselor with just five minutes to spare. She dropped her tote bag down next to a lone black plastic chair in the hallway and sat down. The walls in all the hallways were the same light beige color. There was nothing to look at. Amber guessed they didn't decorate the walls on purpose to show how busy everyone was here. She ate her breakfast and hoped she'd have good news for her parents in a few hours – if she could reach them.

The door to the office opened and her old school teacher appeared.

"Amber Birch?" Mrs. Robertson called and then looked at Amber. "Oh, it's you. I knew that name was familiar. Come on in."

Amber picked up her tote bag and walked in the office. Mrs. Robertson didn't look happy to see her, but maybe she was tired, Amber thought. Everyone was with the long hours they worked.

"Have a seat," Mrs. Robertson said as she sat down herself. She finally smiled at Amber. "I kept hoping I would run into you shortly after you came here, but I never did and then we got busy as workers finished their assignments and were released. I'm sorry I never sought you out. I hope you've been well. How is your family?"

"I'm just fine. It took a while to get used to how things worked here. My family is actually doing well. They're running one of the nearby farms now. I'm hoping to talk to them later today. Alex came with me, though. Do you remember him?"

"Alex McCarthy?"

"Yes."

"I knew Alex well. His mother's sister and I went to college together. They lived near us growing up."

"He's actually one of the reasons I made an appointment with you. I'm hoping to find a way to see him and talk together about what we plan to do with the extension offer. He's working in the auto detail. We've been able to write letters and saw each twice at the summer outings, but there's only one more left and I don't know if he'd be off then."

"Well, I think I just might be able to help you. My husband works at the auto detail. What work cycle are you on?"

"I'm Day C."

"Okay, let me write that down and I'll talk to my husband soon and figure something out. What room number are you?"

"Z273H. Thank you so much! I also wanted to see if you could check how much longer I have to work here for the college option. How exactly does it work when you get close to the end of your commitment?"

"I can look that up for you," Mrs. Robertson got up and went to file cabinets that lined the far wall of her office. She pulled open a drawer and searched through it for a minute and pulled out a piece of paper. "Once you've worked here two years, you can get a full scholarship to a few state schools on the coasts. We encourage those who do this option to try to then work in areas that lost power once they've graduated. The other option is to double the credits your family would get. If you choose college, your family gets the credits you earned during your first year of working. Actually, whenever you leave, the credits would be based on your work. However, the second full year of credits can be exchanged for college or the third year can be exchanged for a car and you get two years of credits.

"Amber Birch started at AmVoc on September 12," she said. "You only have two months left to meet the year commitment. If you want to go to college, we need to start some applications about six months out before the end of the two-year commitment. Let me give you the list of colleges and majors that are approved through this program so you can start thinking that over. Part of the process is also the GED test, but I'm sure you'll have no problems with that. There's some refresher courses on the break room computers and tutors available if you need."

"I actually already completed the GED class and test," Amber said. "I've wanted to go to college to become a teacher since I was a little girl. My parents had to work and went to local community colleges. No one in my family has gone away to college. I'm pretty sure this is the option I want to take, but I do want to talk to my parents about it."

"I understand. Come see me anytime. I'll get with you about seeing Alex soon," she looked up at the clock above her doorway. "Time for my next appointment, though."

"Do you have time to tell me about the extension offer real quick?"

"Oh, yes," Mrs. Roberston said. "If you commit to work a fourth year, a person in your family can get a permanent government job with a bonus of $50,000 worth of credits and a paid off mortgage."

"Thank you, Mrs. Robertson."

"You're welcome, Amber."

Amber left Mrs. Robertson's office and smiled at the boy waiting in the chair. He didn't smile back and looked really tired. His uniform was wrinkled and his brown hair was shiny. She hoped Mrs. Robertson could help him with whatever he was going through. It was tough working here.

Amber headed to the cafeteria but didn't see her friends there. There was only 15 minutes until the update briefing so she headed there. She found Natasha and sat down next to her.

"Any updates?" Natasha asked.

"Yes, actually, but it's a lot. Do you think the guys could meet up with us before dinner?"

"No, they said they have to make a trip to Walter Reed for a checkup for Drew's arthritis. They'll be back for dinner, though."

"Oh, well, I'll tell you what I found out after the briefing and we can catch them up tonight."

Natasha didn't have much time after the briefing until her French class, so Amber caught her up real quick. Natasha looked stunned. She shook her head and told Amber she couldn't believe it. She told Amber the guys hadn't had any calls that week and neither had she, but other people probably had if Amber did.

"Hello?"

"Mom, it's me. I'm so glad I got you on the phone today! I really need to talk to you."

"What's up, Pumpkin?" Amber smiled at mom's old nickname for her.

"It sounds like I only have two months left to go and I can come home or I can stay another year and get a free ride to a state college on one of the coasts. I could work another year for a car instead, or I could come home whenever just with credits. They're also offering a government job, money and a paid off mortgage if I work for four years. What do you think I should do?"

"What do you want to do?"

"I miss home, but I really like the chance to go to college for free. I really think I should take it. But, if you guys need the credits or the car or the mortgage paid off, I'm willing to do what's best for the family."

"Oh, Amber, you're always so sweet. We don't need the credits or car. The farm is producing really well and that stuff is in high demand. We have plenty of credits for the whole neighborhood. We're working on getting more farm equipment, but we really don't need a car. Trucks come to us to pick up the goods or we use the horses if we need to go somewhere. And, we found out that the Snells' old classic car in their garage still works and we can use that in emergencies."

"Really, Mom? It would be so great to go to college after all this. I still want to be a teacher and I'm sure I could find a job near home. I'll try to get home before I go out to school, too."

"We'll probably be able to talk more when you're at college, too," Mom said.

"I do hope so. Is Dad there?"

"Actually, he's outside with Christopher helping get the power back on. They're finally here! I'm inside to let them know when the lights come back on."

"Oh, Mom, finally! I'm so happy for you!" She heard her mom take a sharp breath in.

"It's on," she whispered. "I have to go let them know. I love you, Amber."

"Love you, too, Mom."

Drew was the last person to sit down at their table that evening. He looked worn out. As soon as he sat down, Amber told them about her call and what she found out from Mr. Quinn.

"So, we're back on the investigation?" Scott asked.

"I guess so. I still don't get why Mr. Fray told us it was over if it wasn't," Amber said.

"It's not hard to get confused around here when you're tired," Drew said. "I actually ended up at the work room instead of the cafeteria tonight."

"Are you okay?" Amber asked.

Drew told them about all the tests he had to take that day to see the status of his arthritis. They gave him some medicine when they were done to help with the pain, but he said he still felt really sore.

"Of course, my checkup had to fall on a bad day. My parents actually didn't want me to come back, but I persuaded them to let me by saying Scott would call them if I got worse and would make sure I took my medication," Drew winked at Scott.

"I will call them if you get really bad, but I doubt that will happen," Scott said with a smile.

"So, should we ask your roommate if he's heard anything in the data room again?" Natasha asked Drew, getting back to the food issue.

"I can do that," he said. "Man, I really hope this doesn't get bad again. I dread the calls when moms are crying."

CHAPTER SEVENTEEN

Drew sat down at breakfast the next week and then looked around. He whispered, "My roommate found some information in the data room."

"That was quick," Natasha said. "What did he find?"

"I caught him before he left for shift after we met and asked if he still saw any phone data cards complaining about no food being dropped for a neighborhood. He said that they've been told to give any cards dealing with food supply to their supervisor. He had one last week from Mississippi and when he gave it to his supervisor, he put it into an blue bag in his top desk drawer."

"So, he doesn't collect any data off those cards to put them in the computer system?" Amber asked.

"Nope. He said they weren't getting as many lately, but he used to get three to four each work week," Drew said. "They were told food supply issues were being looked into separately. But, he said when his supervisor put the card in the bag last week, it looked like it was getting pretty full."

"If only we could get that bag," Natasha said.

"I don't think my roommate is up for that," Drew said. "But, he said he would jot down the info of whatever cards he got from now on and pass it on to me."

"It's really sad this is still happening," Amber said. "I wonder why they're saying everything is fine when people aren't getting food. There should be plenty being made out on the coasts."

"I've been thinking about that," Scott piped in. "What if they have enough food, but they're sending more to certain places and less to others? Maybe to their own families?"

Amber shook her head. "That's seriously bad. I hope no one would do that."

"But people are people," Natasha said. "Just because they're working for the government doesn't mean they're good. They had to hire a lot of people to help and there was no way to give everyone background checks like they used to."

"Hey, guys, it's time to go to the briefing," Drew said. "If Scott's right, we need to lay low and not talk too much about this."

"You're right," Natasha said. "Let's resume our book club meetings after the briefings."

Everyone except Amber got up to leave. She wanted to think for just one more minute before going to the briefing. She didn't want to think that someone would really divert food away from those who needed it for their own families, but that's the only reason that really made sense and why it would be covered up. But, how could they prove it?

"Amber, you coming?" Drew said and brought her out of her thoughts.

"Oh, yeah. Thanks. I'm coming," Amber replied and got up from the table to go to follow her friends.

They all got to the meeting room at about the same time after the update briefing a week later and no one spoke a word until the door was closed behind them. Then they all started talking at once.

"I got a phone call ..." Amber said.

"My roommate heard Mr. Quinn ...." Drew said.

"I overheard two men in the hallway ..." Scott said.

"Three phone calls this week ..." Natasha said.

They all stopped. Natasha took charge.

"Okay, let's take turns. Let's start with Drew," she said.

"My roommate told me he heard Mr. Quinn come in

and talk to his supervisor that day – Mr. Fray. He asked why they were still getting calls about the food drops when it was supposedly fixed. He said he didn't think people could be lying on all these calls. Then Mr. Fray looked around the room and took Mr. Quinn to the break room to talk more. When they came out a while later, they were both smiling and laughing. He said they had fifteen calls about food in the past two weeks on his shift."

"I had three," Natasha said. "All in the South."

"I had one in the South, too," Amber said.

"I think I know what's really going on," Scott said. "I actually heard two men talking about food when I left the store this morning to pick up a book. They were right around the corner past our red line. I pretended to read my book and listened. They said that the first time people complained they weren't getting food, a lot of them were lying to try and get extra. They investigated several of the cases and found the people weren't telling the truth. There were a few that had been overlooked because the area had been coded wrong in the system. One of them said the coding was foolproof now so the callers must be lying again. The other guy said, 'Or the coders?' and then they walked off."

"People were lying to get more food?" Drew said incredulously.

"It's hard to be hungry," Natasha growled.

"Oh, sorry," Drew said, his shoulders sinking.

"But, the way the guys said, 'Or the coders?' seems strange to me. Did it sound like he suspected them?" Amber asked.

"Yes, and I do, too," Scott said. "That's my roommate's job and he did say it seemed like a few people on his shift were more buddy-buddy with Mr. Fray than the rest and they seemed to get some extra perks, like longer breaks and it seems like they're able to buy more at the store."

"But, why? Why would you code an area to say it received food when it didn't? It's so wrong!" Natasha said.

"Well, the food has to be going somewhere," Scott said. "If we could find out where it's really going, we could maybe figure out why. But, maybe it's as simple as sending the food to people you care about."

"So, where is Mr. Fray from?" Natasha asked. "I bet it's him."

"I can ask my roommate to check and see if he can trace any extra shipments to that location once we know. I don't know how much he can access after he inputs the data," Drew said.

"Okay, well, let's meet up on the next day off and by then, I think we really have to decide if we're going to do something about this and what. We can't let people go hungry," Amber said. They all agreed and then went to their various classes.

Amber checked the message center first and had a letter from Alex. He apologized for not being able to get to another outing to see her in person before they ended for the summer. He had been sent to Florida again and on their way home, their own truck broke down and he actually got a day off at the nearby beach while it was getting fixed. In a few days he'd be heading to Pennsylvania to do some repair work in various towns around Pittsburgh. He might be gone for three to four weeks. At the end of the letter, he said they actually did leave food in a town in Northern Mississippi where they stayed overnight because they hadn't received any food drops for more than two months. He said he thought she'd want to know after what she had written about in the spring. He'd keep his eye out during their travels to Pennsylvania.

Amber went to the sewing room and let her students just work on whatever project they wanted that day. She answered their questions, but her mind was on the letter from Alex and the phone call home she had today at 5 p.m. Her number was coming up a lot more often now. She guessed it had something to do with seniority. It had now been a year since she'd left home. She really just wanted to hear her parents' voices after all that was going on with the food. She also wanted to see how they were doing with the power back on.

The phone only rang twice before someone picked it up.

"Amber?" her father said.

"Dad! I really hoped someone would be home today. How are you?"

"Doing good," he said. "Sherrie, come here. It's Amber!"

"How's life with power?" Amber asked.

"I have been enjoying having hot water again. We got all new kitchen appliances, too. We just don't have the air conditioning and furnace parts yet, but they should be coming next week."

Amber heard the rustling of the phone changing hands.

"Oh, Amber. I can cook in the kitchen again. And save the leftovers!" her mom exclaimed.

"I'm so glad to hear that. I bet Christopher loves it, too."

"He does. He still works at the farm during the days, but comes home for dinner."

"Everyone else doing good?" Amber asked.

Amber heard dad talk in the background. Their voices were muffled and they went back and forth for a minute.

"Does Dad want something?" Amber finally spoke up. "Have you seen Alex recently?" her mom asked.

"No, he wasn't able to come to the last outing. However, the counselor I talked to, Mrs. Robertson, is going to try and see if he can come visit. Her husband works with Alex. Is everything okay?"

"Not really, Amber. I don't like asking you to tell him, but he hasn't called in a while and his mom wants him to know," her mom paused and her voice caught a little when she started speaking again. "Brian died of a heart attack last week. Nancy tried to revive him for hours, but he was gone."

"Oh no! Not Mr. McCarthy!" tears welled up her eyes. She leaned against the wall of the phone room and started sinking down.

"I know, honey. We still don't have full emergency services up, but we don't know if that would have helped. Will you please tell Alex if you see him? Or have him call home – his mom said he knows their number."

"Amber?" she heard dad's voice now. "Alex's mom is doing okay, but she really misses Alex. I think it would help her a lot if she could talk to him."

"Okay," Amber said through her tears. "I'll find a way to tell him."

"Sorry, honey."

Amber heard a knock on the door to the phone room and was startled. It stopped her tears for a moment. Then, she realized it was because her time was up.

"I have to go now, Mom. My time is up. Tell Mrs. McCarthy I'm so sorry. I'll make sure Alex calls her soon. I love you both very much. Tell Christopher that I love him, too."

"Love you," she heard her dad said in the background.

"I love you so much," her mom said.

"Love you, too."

Amber slowly stood up to hang up the phone and left the phone room. She found a chair nearby and cried quietly. It wasn't unusual to see someone crying outside the phone room. Most people felt a little homesick after calling home. She felt so alone. She couldn't imagine how she would react if her dad had died and Alex had to tell her about it. She'd have to be strong for Alex when she told him, so she spent a while thinking how she would tell him. She hoped her own family would still all be alive by the time she was done working and got back home. There were no guarantees. She missed her family terribly. Would Alex wish he had stayed home and never come to AmVoc? Would she?

CHAPTER EIGHTEEN

Amber was glad the next few work days were fairly easy. She was worried about Alex and kept thinking of how she would tell him. She didn't want to write it in a letter – it would be best in person. But, she couldn't keep it to herself for very long. There was a note taped to her door when she got to her room one night.

> *Amber,*
> *My husband will bring Alex to my office on your next day off first thing in the morning. He can stay a few hours and then they have to leave to fix some vehicles in Pennsylvania. Please come by as early as you can.*
> *See you soon!*
> *Elena Robertson*

Amber smiled and then got nervous. She would have to tell him in two days. She wished it could be someone else giving him the bad news.

Even before breakfast on her day off, she first went and left a note on the sewing room to cancel class for the day. She had told Natasha that she would spending the day with Alex and Natasha said she'd talk to the guys about moving book club to after dinner. She quickly picked out a breakfast burrito and juice from the cafeteria and then went to Mrs. Robertson's office. The door was closed and the lights were off, so she sat in the lone chair and ate her breakfast. She finished eating and read a few chapters of *Little Women* when she heard footsteps coming down the hall. She put her book away and stood up.

"Amber!" Alex said and he started running down the hall to her.

"Alex!" They hugged and then quickly let go since the Robertsons were standing right by them.

"How are you?" Amber spoke up first.

"I'm good. It's nice to be able to come see what the underground section looks like," Alex said.

"It's not that exciting," Amber said.

"Why don't you two go down to the break room so you can catch up? Be back by 2 p.m.," Mrs. Robertson said.

"Sounds good," Alex said. "Are you sure you don't have a swimming pool down here, Amber?"

She laughed. They started walking down the hall.

"Why are they using vehicle maintenance for an intel mission?" She heard Mrs. Robertson ask her husband as they went inside her office. Amber stopped.

"Well, there's another case of food deliveries being reported missing ..." Mr. Robertson said as the door closed.

"Did you hear that?" Amber asked Alex.

"Yes, our next trip isn't about fixing cars at all. Mr. R told me we have to go see if food deliveries are being made at three towns on our way. Guess they've had people lie to get more food and they think it might be happening again. They usually send the repair crews, but there are none in the area, so they're sending us and telling us to tell people we're 'looking for spare parts.'"

"Shhh," Amber said. "We try to be careful. You never know who could be listening."

They walked to the break room and found an empty meeting room. Amber closed the door behind her. She took a deep breath.

"Alex, have you been able to call home recently?"

"No," he said as he sat down in a chair. "Every time I've

tried recently, no one has answered the phone. They purposely don't send us to do work anywhere near our hometowns. I guess a few people have suddenly quit when they got back home. They're having trouble getting more people to volunteer since the power is starting to come back on in most areas now."

"I talked to my parents last week and they wanted me to pass on some news to you," Amber paused. She really didn't want to be the one to tell him. She sat down in the chair next to him and put her hand on his shoulder. She looked into his eyes.

"Alex, your dad died of a heart attack last week."

"What? No ..." Alex stared at her for a minute and then put his head in his hands and slumped down in his chair. He started crying softly. Amber waited a few minutes before she spoke again.

"You might want to see if they'll let you call home today. My parents are back at my house and they can get your mom if no one answers at your house. I'm so sorry, Alex." She kept her arm on his shoulder and let him cry. She had only seen him cry a bit when he got hurt during sports. She felt her eyes welling up, too.

Alex looked up at her after a few more minutes and wiped the tears from his face. Then, he reached over and wiped one from her cheek and held her hand.

"I had a feeling when I left home .... I gave him an extra hug before we left," he said, shaking his head.

They sat in silence for a while longer. Amber wasn't sure what else to say, so she waited for Alex to start talking. Alex finally took a deep breath and started talking.

"I'm so glad you're here, Amber. It's easier to hear bad news with a friend. I'll ask Mr. Robertson about calling home before we head out today. Maybe they can make an exception and let me swing by home on this trip. I can't believe he's gone."

"I hope they do. And, I'm sure Mrs. Robertson would let you call home today," Amber said. "I'm here if you want to talk. "

"Let's talk about something else," he said. She looked at

him to make sure he really wanted to talk about something else. She could tell he was ready for a distraction. Her heart broke for him, though.

"Okay, I wanted to ask you if you thought about the service extension offer? Do you plan on working two or three years here? Or the new four-year plan?"

"I was going to do the extension offer. I really want to get a car out of this deal. But, now I'll probably see if my mom wants me back sooner."

"I did the same thing – I talked to my parents. They're okay without the car. My brother is working on the farm behind the neighborhood now and they use the horses to get around. So, I'm off to college once my two years are up."

"You still want to be a teacher?"

"Yes. I think I'm going to apply to the state colleges in Washington, Florida and Maine. Mrs. Robertson said she'd help me with the applications. My grandma would be so happy to see me go, but it's even better that it will be free. They just want us to try and find jobs in the areas that lost power once we graduate. I'll want to be back home to work anyway."

"Florida sounds nice. I'll let you know what my mom says. I don't know if I want to go away to college anymore. There will be a lot of people needing cars fixed, even if I stay three years. I could open a repair business back home."

"That's not a bad option."

"Hey, what was that about in the hallway earlier? Why don't you want people to know about the food investigation?"

"From what I've been told, there's still the possibility that someone in this compound has something to do with it. Can you tell me what you find out about the food deliveries when you get back? A few of my friends here and I have been getting people call saying they're not getting any food. But then yesterday, I got a call from someone who is getting three a week. It almost seems as if food is getting sent somewhere other than where it should go."

"Wow, that sounds bad."

"I know. It could still be a computer glitch again. But, if we could know for sure it's not people lying again, that would help."

"I can definitely let you know. People shouldn't be going hungry, especially as winter is coming soon. I remember what it felt like when we were low on food and it wasn't even that bad for us."

"I remember, too." Amber looked at the time. "Do you want anything to eat? Or want to play a game of chess while we talk?"

"Can you give me a tour first? Then, let's go get something to eat. I'll be eating MREs the next few days on the road. Let's compare cafeterias."

Amber felt so at ease with Alex there, but it made her even more homesick. She was more stressed now here than she was all that time at home without power. She missed having her family around on the hard days to help support her. The time passed quickly although Alex got really quiet a few times and Amber knew he was thinking about his dad. She wished someone else could have told him, she thought.

They talked while playing chess after lunch and then headed back to Mrs. Robertson's office.

"Right on time," Mrs. Robertson said. "We can try to do this again in a few weeks after they get back."

"Thank you very much," Amber said. "Be safe, Alex. Write me when you get back."

"I will," Alex said. "Thanks for telling me ..."

They hugged for a while and Alex kissed the top of her head again. Then Amber left so Alex could tell the Robertsons about his dad. Mrs. Robertson reached out to put an arm around him and the three of them went into her office. Looks like he would be able to try calling home, Amber thought.

After dinner, she went to meet up with her friends. Natasha and Scott were already in the room. They were working on a crossword puzzle together.

"Where's Drew?" Scott asked Amber.

"I don't know," she replied. Scott looked anxious. "Are you okay?"

"Yeah, I just have a lot to tell you guys, but I don't want

to say it twice."

"Gotcha," Amber said.

"How was Alex?" Natasha asked her as she sat down and started to pull out her notebook. Amber had told her what she had to tell him.

"Not great. That was really hard news to tell. He was going to call his mom this afternoon, though. He actually told me some things I need to tell you guys. Hopefully Drew is here soon."

"Poor guy. I still haven't seen anyone from home since I got here. There were two other girls with me, but I don't know where they got assigned. We weren't that close anyway. My best friend's mom is a single parent, so she stayed to help her."

The door opened and Drew walked in.

"Guys, I have so much to tell you!"

They all looked at him as he shut the door.

"Sounds like we all do," Natasha said. "Let's start with Scott, though, since we left off trying to find out where Mr. Fray is from."

"Kentucky," Scott said. "My roommate was clever and said they were betting on where Mr. Fray's accent was from. He told them Kentucky, but close enough to Cincinnati that he often went there for events."

"No way," Amber said. "That's where I got the call where an MRE delivery fell into a house. No one was hurt, but the lady said they were getting three food drops a week. When I told Mr. Quinn, he said areas were only supposed to get one or two a month."

"It's him, then," Drew said.

"Well, wait," Natasha said. "I don't think we can go with just that. But it does look suspicious."

"I also got two more calls about lack of food from the South this week – one in Tennessee and one in Georgia," Scott said.

"I got one from Mississippi," Drew said.

"Let's add them to the map," Scott said. Amber pulled out her notebook and they added all the new calls.

"They're all in the South and they seem to be scattered

around," Scott said when they were done. There were almost thirty new calls that they could remember between the four of them just over the past two weeks.

"So, we know that some areas aren't getting any food and there's at least one getting more food than they should," Amber said. "My friend said he was going on a trip this week to investigate some of the areas that are calling in but they were doing it undercover saying they are looking for spare vehicle parts. He should be back in a few weeks and he'll let me know what they find out. It sounded like they weren't sure that people were just lying like the first time. They're sending people outside the normal investigative office, so I wonder if they suspect someone on the inside."

"If I wanted to send extra food to my hometown, I would definitely spread out where I was rerouting the shipments from," Drew said. "And, I'd choose the places farthest away so it would take longer to investigate."

Natasha stared at him with a glaring look.

"What? You have to think like a bad guy to catch a bad guy," he said.

"But what if it is just people lying again?" Scott said.

"I would think that more, too, except for that call I got where they had extra food. Now we know there is an area getting more food than it should and it's at least near where someone who works here is from. Mr. Quinn even said something about 'it can't be happening again' when we started getting calls about the lack of food. I'm guessing other people are suspicious if they're sending a vehicle repair crew to investigate instead of the normal people," Amber said.

"Well, maybe we should just let them figure it out," Scott said.

"And let people go hungry? From what I read in the news, the winter is supposed to be colder and snowier than usual, especially in the South. It's already mid-October," Natasha said. "Don't you guys read the news?"

Scott, Drew and Amber looked at anything other than Natasha at that moment.

"That's it – I'm going to start giving you guys news updates every weekend!" Natasha said. Then she touched

Scott's arm. "Do you really trust AmVoc workers who are well-fed and warm to want to work quickly to help the people out there? We need to do something to help move it along."

"I have an idea," Amber said. "But it will probably get one of us in big trouble." She told them her idea and they agreed to think it over and get back with her next weekend. They decided they needed to maintain their distance except during the meetings. They agreed that just one person needed to execute their plan. Who knew what the consequences would be and they didn't want all of them to get in trouble.

"So that's three more from Mississippi, one from Louisiana and one from Florida?" Scott asked as he updated their map on their next day off.

"Plus, there was the weird call I got asking for a supervisor right off the bat," Natasha said. "I managed to get her to at least tell me she was from Kentucky before transferring her to Mr. Quinn. He wasn't on the phone with her long before he moved to the data room."

"Can we really trust Mr. Quinn?" Drew asked. "What if he's working with Mr. Fray?"

"I don't think he is," Amber said. "But it wouldn't hurt to be careful. I'm not sure what AmVoc workers we can trust."

"What about Mrs. Robertson? I saw her this morning to talk about my options. I only have three months left. She seems nice," Natasha said. "Maybe she could help us."

"We might be able to and we might not," Scott said. "If we tell the wrong person, we could all get in trouble and the problem won't get fixed."

"I think we might need to go with Amber's idea, even though I still don't like it," Drew said.

"You all have less time left here than me," Amber said. "And since it was my idea, I think I should be the one to do it."

"Amber, we're all willing. Let's draw straws or sticks or something so it's fair," Natasha said.

"What if we wait until I hear back from Alex and then decide, but not wait any longer than two more work weeks?"

Amber said.

"Sounds good," Scott said. "We can't wait much longer than that or it will be November."

Amber stayed in the room after the other three left and pulled the letter from Alex from her pocket. She couldn't let her friends risk losing their chance to go to college free when they were so close. She had gotten the letter from Alex yesterday and he had confirmed their fear. The people in the South weren't lying this time. The children were hungry and the adults even hungrier. They had turned back after the first two towns to get a semi with food and had given a pallet to each town they passed. They searched several towns for hiding spots, but Alex wrote that there was no way to act that hungry. He wrote about a little boy who took a few ravenous bites after Alex helped him open the MRE and then he turned and hugged Alex for a long time saying "Thank you," over and over.

It was true – there were places where people weren't getting food drops. Food was most likely being rerouted from the South to other places or even just the one place in Kentucky. It had to be stopped. And she knew just how to do it.

CHAPTER NINETEEN

The next weekend, Amber made sure her belongings were packed up neatly in her room. She had a letter to Alex she would drop off in the mailroom before getting breakfast. She also had notes to tack on Drew, Scott and Natasha's doors after she was sure they had left their rooms. She'd do that after breakfast and then head to the briefing. She hoped she was doing the right thing.

Amber found a seat right in the middle of the briefing room. She wanted to be able to say as much as she could before they took her away. The front two rows were filled up with the supervisors, like usual.

"Good morning, shift Day C."

A few people mumbled, "Good morning," back and there was shuffling in the seats as people woke up or put books away.

"The good news keeps pouring in. We are now up to forty percent back up with power. The process should only get easier, so we expect to be at fifty percent within a month. This will be the last winter for anyone without power. We are focusing more food drops to those who will not have power during the winter, although aid will still be given to the entire U.S. The goal is still the same to be at 100 percent on the grid by August of next year. Cars and appliances are being built for distribution and purchase at that time as well.

"There was an outbreak of cholera in Ohio, but with the CDC now fully operational, it was stopped very quickly with only ten deaths in a community of 3,000.

"If anyone has been here more than eighteen months and has not seen a Personal Matters Counselor, please make an appointment soon. We want to make contact with everyone to get decisions made about the extension offer so we know how many people we need to recruit.

"Thank you for your time. That is all today."

"No, that is not all," Amber said in a loud voice as she stood up.

"Excuse me, if you have questions, you need to ..."

"Food isn't getting to everyone," Amber said. "I work in the phone room and there have been numerous calls from people who aren't getting food drops. Still. You said everything was fixed after the people were found lying about not getting food so they could get more, so why is it still happening?

"I think food drops might be being rerouted from someone here. I received a call from a woman who had a food drop make a hole in her roof. She said they had been getting three food drops a week. And they had the power back on. She lives south of Cincinnati, Ohio."

"Who isn't getting food?" she heard someone ask from the back of the room.

"Mainly people in the South. Normally, the South wouldn't have a hard time in the winter, but predictions are for a very cold, snowy winter, there this year."

"Anywhere in Georgia? My family is there!" she heard a boy ask.

"I'm standing up before you all because I don't know if I can trust my supervisor or his supervisor. I need all of you to hear so that something is done to help people. No one should starve this winter, especially if someone is rerouting the food on purpose."

Amber felt a hand on her arm just then and she was being pulled out of her row. Mr. Fray quickly took her out of the room.

"Everyone, please quiet down and sit," the man on the

stage said as she left. "Some people will do anything for attention."

"What are you doing?" Mr. Fray shouted at her as they got into the hallway.

"I'm trying to make sure people don't starve."

He grabbed her arm again and started taking her down the hallway towards an elevator. He used his badge to open it and Amber saw her friends in the hallway coming towards her just as the doors started to close.

"Where are you taking me?"

"You'll see," Mr. Fray said. "Why couldn't you have just let me take care of this?"

"Take care of what?"

"Never mind. Just be quiet for now," he whispered. Then he spoke loudly in the direction of the crowd gathering in the hall, "You'll either be heading home sooner than you thought or going to jail."

Amber recognized the quarantine area when they got close.

"No, you can't put me in here!" Amber said. He quickly opened a door to the farthest room and shoved her in. With no windows or clocks, Amber knew she would lose track of time very quickly if she was there for long. She pounded on the door and screamed for someone to help her, but no one came. She decided to stop and was determined to convince whoever brought her food to let her out. There were a few books and magazines, so she picked an Agatha Christie book and decided to turn a page corner down every time the lights dimmed for night. She found a notepad and some pencils in one of the drawers. She started writing out all that she knew about the food situation. Each time she finished a page, she put it in the back of a magazine. At least if something happens to her, there would be a record of what they knew, she thought.

When the food slot opened hours later she tried asking the person for help, but there was no response. All she could do was wait. What if he told them she had a contagious disease? Or was crazy?

Amber counted four days before the door opened. She

had tried to ask for help every time food was brought to her, but no one answered her. She stayed sitting on the bed when the door opened. Mr. Fray walked in and closed the door behind him. Amber just glared at him.

"I am sorry I had to leave you in here for so long," he started. "It was for your own safety."

"Mine? I'm guessing you were just protecting yourself."

"Hear me out and then you can pass judgment. Okay?"

She crossed her arms and leaned back against the wall.

"We've been investigating these food drops for a while now and were finally convinced it had to be someone here rerouting the food. We've suspected Mr. Quinn for a while now – actually, several of us have. We suspected him during the first round of missing food drops, but never found any evidence that he was rerouting food to another location. When it started happening again, we wanted to find hard evidence. We thought he maybe paid off the people in the towns to lie about lying, so we sent some people from the vehicle maintenance team to go to the towns and look around. Your friend Alex was part of that – Mr. Robertson told me. He is working with me.

"That call you got about the food falling into the roof was a key development. However, your announcement got us the evidence we needed. As you were speaking, Mr. Quinn left the briefing room. He tried going through the cafeteria to use their service elevator, but your friends had noticed him leaving and followed him. They found him cornering a cafeteria worker trying to get her badge to use the elevator. Your friends shouted at him and distracted him. When he turned around, the cafeteria worker kicked him and he fell. She ran out to tell her supervisor what was happening and he was taken away."

"Who was the cafeteria worker?" Amber had to ask.

"Jessie Bryman. Do you know her?" Amber just smiled and nodded.

"Why didn't you come get me then?"

"We went through Mr. Quinn's room and found documents that he was working with a few other people. We've been finding all of the accomplices to make sure they didn't try to retaliate against you and we've been deciding what to do with you," he said. He finally stopped pacing and looked straight at her. "Several people just want to make this go away quietly and send you home. However, your friends came to me and explained how much effort you all have been putting into this and why."

"We just wanted to make sure people didn't go hungry this winter," Amber said. "I remember what it was like. Natasha went through worse before she came here."

"We know that all now. I'm here to take you to your room to change and then we're going to today's briefing. You and your friends are going to be recognized for the work you've done."

"Recognized? Like an award?"

"Something like that. You'll see. Let's get going. We only have forty-five minutes and I think you'll want to shower."

Mr. Fray took her to her room and waited outside while she got ready. In the briefing room, there was standing room only. Mr. Fray took her up to the front where her friends were sitting in chairs facing the audience. There was an empty chair for her. Natasha was the first to jump up and hug her.

"We were worried about you!"

"They said you were somewhere safe, but they wouldn't tell us where," Scott said.

"They stuck me in a quarantine room."

"Did they give you all the details about Mr. Quinn?" Drew asked her.

"Just now. Mr. Fray came to get me, but I didn't hear from anyone since I was here last."

"That's horrible! We were stuck in Mrs. Robertson's room, but they at least kept us informed about what was going on," Natasha said.

"I need you guys to take your seats," Mr. Fray told them as he approached the podium in the front of the room. They sat down and the room got quiet.

"Good morning, shift Day C. I know many of you have been wondering what happened to the girl who spoke out at the last briefing and if what she said was true. I have heard from several of you who have family in the South and it turns out you were right to be concerned. What Amber Birch said a few days ago was true. Several people at this facility were working with Jared Quinn to reroute food drops to locations where they had family and friends. This has been stopped and extra food has already been delivered to the locations that missed food drops."

A few murmurs went up in the room.

"How can we know for sure? This happened before," said a boy in the back of the room.

"I completely understand your lack of trust. We will have people at the doors and if you have family in the South, you will be given the chance to call home today to check with your family.

"In the end, we have to give some credit to Ms. Birch and her friends for being persistent when they saw a serious problem. These four, with the help of their roommates – who will be recognized during their shift – realized that people would starve this winter if they didn't get the food drops they were promised. They were not going to stop until the problem was solved. Amber, Natasha, Jessie, Andrew and Scott – please stand.

"These five will have the option of going home in two weeks with the credits earned by three years of service. It is a small thank you from the many people in the South who will now survive this winter."

Everyone stood up and applauded. Amber looked at her friends and they smiled. Going home meant the world to all of them. Amber wondered if she could start college in January instead of waiting until the fall.

The applause ended and they sat down. Mr. Fray gave the rest of the briefing and then dismissed the room.

"We get to go home!" Natasha said.

"With a car and college, too!" Drew said.

"I hope I can start classes in January," Amber said. "We'll have to talk with Mrs. Robertson about our options."

Mr. Fray walked over to them and put his hand on Scott's shoulder.

"We need you guys to work one more week. There are a

few people finishing up training this week that can then take your spots. Then, we'll do your debriefing week and get you home. Mrs. Robertson is expecting all of you at 2 p.m. to discuss your future plans. I'll see you at work tomorrow."

Mrs. Robertson had them all sit around her desk and talk about their options. Jessie had asked to go back to work and talk to Mrs. Robertson the next day. They would each get a car and credits for their family to use for appliances and then either a college scholarship, training, a job or a stipend for four years. They had to apply to colleges, but Mrs. Robertson assured them it was just a formality. AmVoc was assured a few spots at every state college on the coasts. If they chose college, they could go home first until the next semester started in January.

"Apply to two or three, though. Sometimes we come across a college that is absolutely full or that wants to end their agreement with us," Mrs. Robertson told them. "If you need to call home first, we can do that now, too."

"I'd like to try to talk to my parents first," Drew said.

"Me, too," Natasha said.

"Okay, let's go next door to make the calls. Natasha, you come first," Mrs. Robertson said.

"You don't need to call home, Scott?" Amber asked.

"No. I know my parents want me to go to college. My Dad actually went to UCLA, so I'll apply there and maybe another in California," Scott said. "You already know what you want to do?"

"Yes, I talked to my parents after they offered the extension. They want me to go to college, too. My grandmother used to remind me to 'Study hard – college awaits!' every time she said goodbye. Both my parents had to work their way through college. They want me to get the full experience."

Natasha came back in and sent Drew in to the next room. She had a big smile on her face.

"They said to go for it! I had never thought of going to college before working here. I would have had to get scholarships or work. I want to apply as close to home as I can get, though," Natasha said.

Drew came back in just then. Mrs. Robertson had her hand on his shoulder.

"Everything okay?" Amber asked him.

"No one answered the phone," Drew said. "I'll have to try again later. I don't think they'll want me going away for a long time, but I guess I can apply just in case, right?"

"Yes. I can always tell them you changed your mind, but if you apply, at least it will be an option," Mrs. Robertson said.

All four of them applied to a few different colleges. Natasha stuck with Virginia and New York. Drew chose Arizona and Washington. Scott went with California schools. Amber applied to Florida and Maine. They had to fill out personal information, the grades they remembered, activities done during their time in AmVoc and a short essay about what they wanted to achieve in life.

When they were all done, Mrs. Robertson walked with them to the cafeteria for dinner. They walked in and were hit in the face with streamers and cheering noises.

"It's a party – for you," Mrs. Robertson said.

They all stood there for a few seconds to take it all in and then scattered about. Amber was tired and hungry, so she went over to get some pizza. Someone came and stood right beside her.

"So, Amber, what are you going to do?"

She turned and saw Alex standing beside her.

"Alex!" She turned and hugged him. "I'm so glad to see you. Can you believe all this?"

"Yes, but I still can't believe you were brave enough to speak up during a briefing. What you did is all over the place and the news!"

"I would never have done it if not for your letter. I knew something drastic had to be done and I didn't know whom I could trust. I figured there would be at least one adult who would look into what I said. Plus, I couldn't let my friends risk getting in trouble – they didn't have as much time left here on their commitments."

Alex picked out some pizza, too, and then found a seat a little away from the big crowd in the cafeteria.

"Looks like they have cake over there, too," Alex said. "But, really, did you decide what you're going to do? They gave me the same offer since I was part of the investigation. I was actually already applying to leave early to go be with my mom, but Mr. Roberston talked to his wife to help me out."

"I applied to a couple colleges, but I get to go home for a bit first. We have to work one week and then we get a debriefing week."

"Same here! With the work and debriefing at least. Maybe we'll get the same ride home."

"I hope so. Are you still planning on staying home, though?"

"Well, I talked to my mom. I really don't want to go away to college, but she thought I would need something to help me set up my own repair shop. So, I'm going to do some auto mechanic training and business classes. They have some in Virginia. She said my dad would be proud."

Alex looked down and Amber took his hand.

"He would be proud of you." Amber whispered. "I like your plan, too, Alex. There will definitely be lots of cars needed repairs soon. I guess my parents will give up the horse and wagon at some point."

"I can't wait to see that!"

"What a world, huh?"

They got some cake and then talked about what they would do when they got home. It didn't feel like hardly any time passed when someone announced it was time to get back to their rooms.

"See you soon," Amber told Alex when they said goodbye.

"Very soon."

CHAPTER TWENTY

For Amber, debriefing reminded her of quarantine week. It was pretty much lounging around waiting until your ride home was lined up. They played a lot of Monopoly. Natasha left first. There was a group heading to a factory that was set to re-open in her hometown just a week after they set things up with Mrs. Robertson.

"You promise you'll write?" she asked them as they gathered to say goodbye.

"We will," Amber replied. Natasha gave them each a hug and then turned around. She didn't look back. Amber doubted she'd be able to do the same.

The day before Natasha left, Drew and Scott finally got a message from their parents. They wouldn't be able to pick them up for another month, but then both their families would be going home. They decided they would pick up a few work shifts until they left, but they set their schedules so they only worked every other day.

Amber was scheduled to leave three days after Natasha. Drew and Scott had made sure to have that day off to say goodbye. The day before she left, she spent the day buying some gifts for her family, cashing out her account, writing messages to her sewing students and cleaning up the sewing room.

She was reading *The Hobbit* during lunch when someone sat down across from her.

"I just heard you were leaving tomorrow," Jessie said.

Amber hadn't seen her since the party. "I'm glad I caught you before you left."

"Me, too! I really wanted to give you my address so we could stay in touch."

"Are you going to stay at home or go to college?"

"I'm heading to college, but I don't know where yet. I'm hoping for Florida."

"I did, too, but to culinary school. I have two more weeks and then there's a convoy heading down there."

"That would be fantastic!"

Jessie had to get back to work, but she gave Amber a big hug before she left.

"Thanks for being so brave," she said.

"Thanks for being my friend," Amber replied.

Amber was surprised to see Alex sitting at a table in the cafeteria when she went to dinner that night. She had been hoping they could go home together but she hadn't heard from him for a few days.

"I got us the best ride home," Alex said before she could sit down.

"Do we get to fly?" Amber asked. She had never been on a plane.

"Nope. Try again."

"Train?"

He pulled some keys out of his pocket and jangled them in front of her.

"I get to drive my car home," he said. "And, you're coming with me."

"Just us?"

"Just us."

They left early the next morning after saying goodbye to Drew and Scott at breakfast. Mrs. Robertson stopped by to say goodbye, too. Alex drove carefully and even let Amber drive for a while on a straight highway. There was only one checkpoint on their way and Alex had all the proper paperwork. They had to go slower a few times at places where cars were still scattered on the roadway. There was always a path, but it was sometimes narrow. Just wide enough for a military truck to get through, Amber thought. Neither of them had to be at class until January, so they had two months to enjoy being home. They spent the entire ride swapping stories from their time at AmVoc and talking about what they were excited to do when they got home. They didn't talk about Alex's dad, but Amber could tell when he was thinking about him.

They were able to make the drive in one day and got home just as the sun was setting. Alex parked on the street right between their houses. As soon as he turned the car off, they looked at each other and Alex squeezed her hand.

"We're home!" They both smiled and then quickly left the car. They each ran to their front doors with big smiles on their faces. Amber heard Alex's mom cry out his name right before she opened her own door.

"Mom? Dad?"

"Amber? Is that you?"

"It's me. Alex got to drive us home, so we got to come straight here." Amber barely finished her sentence before he parents engulfed her in a hug. They all started crying tears of mostly joy.

"We'll go see Christopher first thing in the morning," Dad said. "He's been staying at the farm at nights to help with the harvest. They're up early and stay up late."

Amber noticed they had a lamp on in the living room and heard the quiet hum of a refrigerator working in the kitchen. She walked in and turned on the kitchen faucet. Water came out.

"It's almost like it was before," she said.

Mom came up and put her arm around her.

"Almost, except all you kids have had to grow up so much," she said. "Jack, can you go get her bags from the car?"

"I have so much to tell you guys," Amber said to her mom.

"I bet you do! They called us to tell us what you and your friends did. We're so proud of you. Are you really, truly doing okay, though?"

Amber took a minute before answering.

"I am. It was scary at some parts, but now that I'm

home, it mainly feels surreal."

Amber's dad came back in with her bags and gave her another big hug.

"Guess what we've been saving to have for dinner when you got home?" Dad asked her.

"What?"

"Bacon cheeseburgers and ice cream – we'll have it tomorrow when Christopher can come, too."

"Sounds perfect!"

Amber sat with her parents in the living room for the next hour and they shared stories until Amber started yawning. Miss Gray had sat in her lap the whole time, too, purring away.

"I bet you need some sleep. We'll get you all caught up in the morning. Your room is all made up for you. I put it together right after you called two weeks ago," her mom said.

"Okay. Love you guys."

"We love you, too, Amber," her mom said.

"So glad you're home," her dad said.

Two months passed by quickly. The weather turned cold and snowy quickly and there were still problems with a lot of furnaces. Each house had a space heater to use, so Amber and her parents often slept together in their bed like they did when the power was out the first winter. Alex decided to make sure he got trained on appliance repair, too, after being home. There was a lot of repair work to do, chores to help her brother with at the farm and weekly food drops to distribute. Amber spent many days repairing clothing for the neighborhood. The farm was definitely in good shape and that made Amber feel more comfortable heading off to college. Once she graduated, she would find a job at one of the local schools and help at the farm so her brother could take some agriculture classes. The demand for food was so high across the country, the farm would support her family for a long time. Christopher was even talking with the other farmers in the area to work together over the next few years. Her little brother seemed very grown up to her now.

In early December, Amber got a phone call from AmVoc telling her she had been accepted to the University of Florida. She would need to be back at AmVoc on January 3 to catch a flight or find her own way out to the school. Alex had to be in class by January 7, so he couldn't drive her all the way to Florida and be back in time but he could drive her to AmVoc. He had taught her how to drive while they were home, but she decided to wait and get a license when she was in Florida. Plus, Alex told her to wait and pick up her earned car when she was out on the coast. The cars from out there tended to be more reliable. She would try to get one by spring break so she could drive home in the summer, unless she took summer classes. She wanted to enjoy college, but also finish and get back home as soon as she could. After spending almost two years away from home, she knew that home was where she wanted to be.

"Hey, be safe while you're out there, okay?" Alex said as he helped her take her bag out of the trunk after they got to AmVoc.

"I will," Amber said and then laughed. "Although, after all we've been through, college should be a breeze."

"Very true!" Alex replied as he laughed, too. He gave her a hug and then held her hand for a minute.

"Call me soon, okay? And, come back," he looked up in her eyes. "I'll miss you."

Amber smiled and squeezed his hand. He leaned in and kissed her. They had a connection that really couldn't be explained to anyone other than those who survived without power and then spent time at AmVoc.

"I'll miss you, too, Alex," she said, smiling. "I promise – I will come back."

She flew in a military plane to Florida with a few other people her age, but mostly soldiers. They were headed to Florida for training, but couldn't tell her what kind. They mostly seemed tired, so she just read the whole flight.

"When we land, please let the military get off first and then we will get the civilians to their locations," a voice came of the speaker and said. There were only six people left on the plane after the military got off.

"McGuire, Jensen, Bennet and Turner, please come forward." Those four were led off the plane.

"Birch and McComb, please come forward." Amber and the only other teenager left followed the man who had called their names. "Please get into the third car – the red one. Your luggage is already in the trunk. You are both headed to the University of Florida."

Amber and Callie McComb ended up being roommates. Callie had heard of what Amber did at AmVoc. She worked in the cafeteria for two years and knew Jessie. They were both in the teaching program, too. They had one day to get settled followed by an orientation day and then classes started. They stuck together since they both understood what each other had been through. In orientation, they asked everyone to introduce themselves. Only those from the Midwest specified how long they had lived without power. Out of the sixty-five new students, only seven were from the Midwest. Amber was last for introductions.

"Hi, my name is Amber Birch. I've always dreamed of going to college and becoming a teacher. I'm from North Carolina and lived through life with no electricity for a year and a half. Then I spent almost two years working for the government for the restoration. I'm so glad to be here."

"Are you the Amber Birch?" the professor in charge of orientation asked as he removed his glasses and looked at her closely. "The one who discovered the food problem in the South?"

"My friends and I did," Amber said. He walked over to her and reached out to shake her hand.

"Thank you," he said. "My aunt and uncle live in Alabama." All of the students started talking to each other and several came over and talked to her about what she did. She said she just did what she thought was right – everyone had to take care of each other.

Acknowledgments

I can't thank my husband and daughters enough for how many times they helped me reach for my dreams.

Thank you to Conlan Slaney and Fiona Phillips for your early reading of this book and your feedback.

ABOUT THE AUTHOR

Sarah Anne Carter is a lover of books. She is an avid reader and is a book review blogger. Writing stories since she was little, she is constantly thinking of ideas that could be used as a plot for a novel. She is a journalist by trade and has written numerous newspaper articles. She grew up as an Air Force brat and married a military man and has lived in many states and countries. Currently residing in Ohio, she spends her time enjoying her family, reading and writing. *Life After* is Sarah Anne's second published novel. Her first novel, *The Ring*, was published in 2019.

Want to know more? You can reach Sarah Anne at her Web site at **www.sarahannecarter.com**.

Please take the time to leave a review of *Life After* on Amazon, Goodreads or wherever you review books!

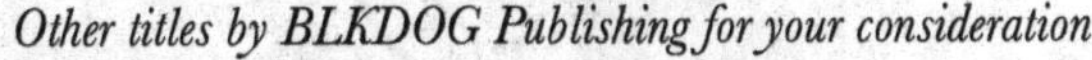

Other titles by BLKDOG Publishing for your consideration

The Ring
By Sarah Anne Carter

A story of love, loss and hope.

Amanda knows three things about her life – she loves living in Tacoma, she wants to be a teacher and she will never marry a man in the military. Yet, when Lucas comes into the coffee shop where she works wearing a flight suit, he starts to change her mind about her future. She is determined to just be his friend, but the chemistry between them is undeniable and their relationship survives through two deployments and him being on work trips almost half of the time.

After they get married, they move across the country to Charleston, S.C., and Amanda finds a job, which helps somewhat with the loneliness of Lucas being gone a lot. She thought she was prepared for life as a military wife, but then she starts finding out the true sacrifices military families make.

Arc City Stories
By various authors

Welcome to Arc City.

Arc City is a city that exists in a world beyond governments, where war and climate change have destroyed the old order. Corporations are now the authorities of the surviving city-states. The elite live in luxury above the clouds in their towers; everyone else lives further down, based on their corporate and economic worth.

Arc City Stories is an exciting, action-packed collection of nine cyberpunk tales, written by eight authors, of various citizens each trying to survive, in their own way, in this brave new world.

Consumed
By Justin Alcala

Sergeant Nathaniel Brannick is trapped in Victorian London during a period of disease, crime and insatiable vices. One night, Brannick returns from work to find an eerie messenger in his flat that warns him of dark things to come.

When his next case involves a victim who suffered from consumption, he uncovers clues that lead him to believe the messenger's warning. Despite his incredulity, he can't help but wonder if the practical man he once was has been altered by an investigation encompassed in the paranormal. That is, until he meets the witch hunters, and everything takes a turn for the worse.

Prester John: Africa's Lost King
By Richard Denham

He sits on his jewelled throne on the Horn of Africa in the maps of the sixteenth century. He can see his whole empire reflected in a mirror outside his palace. He carries three crosses into battle and 100,000 men guard each cross. He was with St Thomas in the third century when he set up a Christian church in India. He came like a thunderbolt out of the Far East eight centuries later, to rescue the crusaders clinging on to Jerusalem. And he was still there when Portuguese explorers went looking for him in the fifteenth century.

He went by different names. The priest who was also a king was Ong Khan; he was Genghis Khan; he was Lebna Dengel. Above all, he was a Christian king who ruled a vast empire full of magical wonders: men with faces in their chests; men with huge, backward-facing feet; rivers and seas made of sand. His lands lay next to the earthly Paradise that had once been the Garden of Eden.

Was he real? Did he ever exist? This book will take you on a journey of a lifetime, to worlds that might have been, but never were. It will take you, if you are brave enough, into the world of Prester John.

EST. 2019
BLKDOG